UNDER HER SKIN

LINDI PARKER, SHIFTER SHIELD
BOOK ONE

MARGO BOND COLLINS

Under Her Skin
Copyright © 2016 by Margo Bond Collins

Published by Bathory Gate Press
Texas

BATHORY GATE
—— P R E S S ——

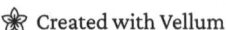 Created with Vellum

About Under Her Skin

Lindi Parker works hard at being human, not an easy task for a snake shifter. She has no desire to search for others like her—until a new case changes everything.

When Lindi learns that she's not the only shapeshifter in the world, she realizes she might be next on a killer's list.

In order to save herself and the abused children she works with, she will have to team up with Dr. Kade Nevala, a member of the shifter tribe responsible for eradicating weresnakes—and the most attractive man Lindi's ever met.

Even more terrifying, she'll need to embrace her serpent side, a choice that has enormous consequences for Lindi, and for everyone around her.

CHAPTER
ONE

"Some sons-a-bitches just need killing." Detective Daniel Moreland stared down at the body of the man sprawled across the bedroom floor and shook his head. Blood puddled on the hardwood floor and spattered the pink gingham bedspread. It made me dizzy to look at it, so I stared at the detective instead.

I hadn't realized that I would be able to smell the blood quite so clearly—something the humans around me hadn't known they would need to mention.

"Where's the girl?" I asked.

He jerked his head toward the front of the house. "Outside. EMTs have her in the ambulance."

"Anyone talked to her yet?"

He shook his head. "Just me—and only long enough to get her out to the bus."

I nodded. "I'll join her, then."

He grunted noncommittally and I turned toward the door, my movements jerkier than I would have preferred—I wanted to pretend that being at a crime scenes didn't bother me, but it did.

"Hey, Lindi." Moreland reached out and touched my sleeve. "You see anything. . . ." He paused for a moment, looking around the pink-and-white bedroom as if it might provide the words he was looking for. "You know. Weird?"

I stared into his eyes for a long moment, a frisson of fear shivering its way across my spine.

What does he know?

Finally, I shook my head. "Why?" I asked.

He bit his bottom lip. "Not sure. We haven't found the murder weapon yet," he said. "Just thought maybe you might have some insight."

"I don't see anything weird. Just some son-of-a-bitch who needed killing," I said softly.

He looked into my eyes for a moment longer, then dropped his hand to his side. "Yeah," he said, just as quietly. "There is that. Go on. See to the girl."

OUTSIDE THE HOUSE, red and blue lights flashed on the yard, almost blinding me. Neighbors clustered along the sidewalk, their comments and whispers a faint buzz in the night. I licked my lips, surreptitiously tasting the air as I walked toward the ambulance. The copper tang of blood from the house overwhelmed almost everything else, but I tasted an undertone of fear and anger. The scents from the crowd were almost electric on my tongue—their eagerness for news of someone else's disaster hummed across the air, heightening my shapeshifter senses.

The heat of the August day hadn't dissipated with nightfall—it rarely does, in Texas—and I could almost see it rising in waves from the asphalt of the street.

It took serious concentration to overcome my desire to sink down, curl up, and soak in the warmth.

Moving into professional mode, I stepped into the rectangle of light cast by the open doors of the ambulance.

Normally I wouldn't be at an actual murder scene, but a new grant for a community initiative program provided for a counselor from the Child Advocacy and Protection Center —the CAP-C—to work with children present at a potentially traumatic crime scene. Tonight was my night on duty, the first time since the initiative took effect that I got called out. Lucky me.

Ten-year-old Emma Camelli was pretty much certain to be traumatized.

The dead man in her bedroom was her father.

And she was the one who had killed him.

The little girl huddled in the middle of the gurney at the back of the ambulance looked too frail to have stabbed an adult male to death. But the drying blood on her hands and soaking the front of her *Frozen* pajamas belied that frailty. Her dishwater blonde hair hung in hanks around her thin face and she looked up at me, her blue eyes filled with tears.

A uniformed officer I hadn't met before stood outside the ambulance, her hands looped into her belt. I nodded to her and introduced myself. "Lindi Parker. I'm the counselor."

The officer looked me up and down appraisingly, her eyes cool. "Joanna Ashford. Moreland told me to watch for you." Her voice was surprisingly soft and high. "I'll be right here if you need me."

"You guys got everything you need from her?" I asked.

Ashford shrugged. "Not yet. She'll get checked out at the hospital as soon as you give us the go-ahead to leave. CSU will get her clothes and scrape underneath her nails and all that there."

I hadn't realized that I would get to talk to her before

3

the techs gathered evidence. Still, I was glad—at least this way I'd be able to let her know what was coming.

I slung myself up into the ambulance. Emma watched me, her lips compressed. She sat cross-legged on the gurney with her arms crossed in front of her.

"Hi," I said, sitting down on the bench across from her.

She didn't answer.

When I first started my training, I often tried to convince kids to talk to me. I have discovered over the years, however, that silence is generally a better motivator than questions, at least initially.

So I crossed my arms to mirror Emma's pose and leaned back against the vehicle wall, waiting, watching the little girl.

The silence stretched out. Emma uncrossed her arms and started picking at something on her leg—I couldn't tell if it was a scab or dried blood from her dead father.

I uncrossed my arms and dropped them into my lap. Emma glanced at me out of the corner of her eye.

I counted the seconds in my head—a good way to keep myself occupied while waiting for the girl to speak.

Sixty.

Ninety.

Finally, Emma couldn't take the silence any longer.

"I told him I'd do it," she said sullenly. She stared at her feet.

"Do what?" I asked, my voice mild. I maintained my casual pose.

"Kill him." She cut her eyes toward me, gauging my reaction.

"Hm." I let the silence stretch for a moment, then spoke again. "How come?"

She shrugged. But she'd started talking, so I could probably get the story out of her now. I leaned toward her, my elbows on my knees so that my hands dangled between my legs.

"Did he do something that made you mad?"

She nodded.

I let the silence stretch out again.

Emma's brow furrowed and she looked up at me through her hair. "You don't want me to tell you?" she asked.

I shrugged. "Only if you want to."

She pursed her lips and picked at her leg again.

I only made it to forty-seven before she spoke, this time in a whisper.

"He hurts me."

"When did he hurt you, Emma?" I asked, purposely using the past tense to counteract her use of the present—he couldn't hurt her anymore.

Her shoulders hunched in on themselves, making her look even more fragile. "Every time Momma goes out of town."

"Does your momma go out of town a lot?" I asked.

A nod. "Every two weeks." I could barely hear her, she spoke so quietly.

I breathed in slowly through my nose, willing myself to bury the anger rising through me—I could deal with it later, after I'd helped Emma.

Her jaw tightened. "I told him," she said. "I told him not to touch me anymore. I told him and he didn't listen, so I hurt him."

"How did you hurt him, Emma?" I asked gently.

"Like this." She stabbed one of her hands straight out in front of her, palm down, fingers pointed away from her. Her back had straightened and she no longer looked frail. Her eyes were narrowed and her mouth twisted in a snarl. She looked feral.

"What did you use to kill him?" I asked.

She turned toward me, confused. "My hand." Her tone suggested that perhaps I was more than a little slow.

"But what was in your hand?" I asked.

"My hand. I just *changed* it," she said.

I froze. "Changed it?" I asked, my voice carefully neutral. "How did you change it?"

She tilted her head and looked at me. "You know. I thought about it. And then it changed."

"What did it look like when it changed?" I asked.

"Like a knife," she said. "Only all black and shiny. When I change, I get a hard skin. Not like you," she continued. "When you change, you go all wiggly."

My breath caught in the back of my throat.

How does she know what happens when I shift?

I started to ask, but Moreland stuck his head in through the door. "We're about to leave, Lindi. The mom called and is meeting us at the hospital as soon as she can."

"Brinks Children's?"

"No. Kindred Hospital." Moreland shrugged. "The mom insisted."

I nodded and stood up, preparing to hop back out of the ambulance and follow Moreland as he walked away.

Emma's quiet voice stopped me.

"It's where all the shifters go."

CHAPTER
TWO

I sat in my car, hands gripping the steering wheel in front of me. The entrance to the Kindred Hospital glowed a fluorescent white in the darkness. I'd never been inside, never thought I'd had a reason to.

My adoptive parents taught me early on to avoid anything that might give me away—medical exams were not a possibility, so I never went to a hospital. They home-schooled me until I was twelve and they were sure I had my shifting under control so I could go to school with other children.

I don't know how old I was when Dad found me. He's a biology professor who specializes in snakes—a herpetologist who brought home what he thought was an adolescent individual of a new species, a snake that flared its hood like a cobra. He was stunned to find a toddler curled up in the tank the next morning, and even more surprised when he actually saw me shift from one form to another.

Finding a new breed of snake would have made him famous, at least among certain circles.

Finding a weresnake made him a father.

My knuckles turned white as I tried to convince myself to go inside the hospital. There might be answers in there. But I wasn't sure I wanted answers.

I jumped at a sharp rap on the window. Moreland leaned in as I rolled it down.

"You coming?" he asked.

"Yeah." I grabbed my purse and hung it over my shoulder, then took a deep breath and followed the detective inside.

Most hospitals smell the same: of antiseptic, saline, medicine, with an undertone of death. Another smell underlay those here; something sharp and new to me.

Shapeshifters, maybe?

A small, dark-haired nurse met us outside Emma's room. The girl lay in the bed, staring up at the ceiling.

"The doctor will be here momentarily to speak to her," the nurse said quietly, "and then I'll do a rape kit. You're the counselor?" She turned to me.

I nodded. "Lindi Parker. Do you want me to talk to her about the kit?"

"That might be helpful. I've already spoken to her, but she might need to hear it again." She moved further out into the hall with Moreland.

Emma glanced at me as I entered the room, then back up at the ceiling.

"Hi, Emma. You know what's going to happen here?" I asked, working to keep my voice gentle.

Emma's brow furrowed. "I don't want to talk about it."

A deep voice interrupted from the doorway. "I'd like to hear, too, Emma."

I glanced up and drew in a breath to speak, to encourage Emma to verbalize what she knew, but the words never left my mouth.

Emma's doctor stood framed in the doorway, a half-smile arrested on his face, his light brown eyes wide as he stared at me in shock.

The smell of him filled the room—almost spicy, and utterly terrifying. I froze, but the muscles under my skin rippled. Sucking in air, I flicked my tongue out across my lips. His scent flowed through my mouth. He tasted like heat, but not like prey. Like a threat.

He smelled like danger, and I was about to shift.

Oh, hell.

The room swung into shades of gray and I blinked quickly to keep him from seeing the slitted pupils of my partially shifted eyes.

I closed my mouth and breathed deeply through my nose, focusing on my mammal senses, the human part of me. I glanced down at the floor and waited for the colors to come flooding back. Once I was in control of myself, I looked back up at him.

With a shudder that trembled through his entire body, he shook himself out of his immobility.

The whole thing couldn't have lasted for more than a few seconds, but I was drenched in sweat.

"Hi, Emma." His voice was calm, but his hand trembled as he reached up to adjust the stethoscope hanging around his neck.

"Hi, Dr. Nevala," Emma said.

This was where all the shifters went, she had said. Clearly, she already knew the doctor.

He moved closer to her and I backed away, making sure I never turned my back on him. He busied himself listening to her chest and murmuring to her. The familiar tasks apparently steadied him and his own shaking stopped.

I stepped out of the room and leaned against the wall right outside the door, trying to calm my racing heart.

What just happened in there?

Brushing my hair back off my forehead, I straightened, taking a deep breath and blowing it back out. The nurse turned the corner and headed back into the room.

I need to go back—it's my job to help Emma through this.

But my heart was still thudding and my mouth tasted like copper and fear.

Dad always said that I should remember that I was a person first—that whatever else I might be, I was human. His lessons had helped me learn to control my shifting. I ignored the other part of me as much as I could, keeping it pushed as far under my humanity as possible.

I can control it now, too.

But I felt the muscles of my back rippling as my body tried to fight me.

"You okay?" Moreland's voice made me jump.

"Yeah. Fine. Just a little rough in there," I said.

"Always is with the kids." He shook his head. "I've got a uniform coming to stay with her until the mom gets here. Tomorrow, if the doctor okays it, we'll start moving her through the family court system, figure out what to do with her."

I bit my lip. "I believe her, Dan. What she said to me, her body language, all of it was congruent. I think she was being sexually assaulted."

"Then we'll get her help," he said. "That's why you're on the team." He put a hand on my shoulder and squeezed lightly, silent support flowing through the touch and calming me.

"I need to go sit with her while they do the kit," I said, as a uniformed officer stepped around the corner. Moreland waved an acknowledgment at me as he moved to meet the other policeman.

I took a bracing breath and stepped back into the room.

Dr. Nevala was still talking to Emma. He tensed when I entered, but he didn't look up at me.

Now that I wasn't overcome with sheer physical terror, I could see that he didn't loom over me, as I had first thought. He couldn't have been more than an inch or two over my own 5'7". But he had enough presence to fill up the tiny hospital room. Emma and the nurse both seemed enthralled by him.

I leaned against the wall, willing myself still.

"Okay, Emma," Nevala said. "In a minute, I'll do the swab, just like we discussed."

Emma's eyes flickered over to me.

"Would you like me to hold your hand?" I asked.

"Yes, please." She spoke softly.

Nevala stiffened at the sound of my voice, but his hands were gentle on the child. She clutched my fingers while he completed the exam, but she never even whimpered.

The doctor didn't look at me as he said goodbye to Emma and walked away.

I PULLED out my smartphone as soon as I left the hospital room.

As awful as sitting with Emma had been, focusing on my job had calmed my nerves after Nevala had left.

I opened my notes file and began tapping away, taking down my impressions before I forgot them. The uniformed officer standing outside the doorway nodded as I walked by. Though I had worked with him before, I couldn't remember his name.

The exam had been unpleasant, of course, but Emma had held up well. The nurse had given her a mild sedative. I had left Emma sleeping, after making sure both she and the nurse had a copy of my card.

I hadn't had another chance to talk to her alone. I didn't know what I would have said, anyway, didn't know where to start discussing something that had been my biggest secret all my life. Wasn't sure discussing my shapeshifting with a traumatized child was anything I was willing to do.

So instead, I focused on work. It was late, almost two in the morning. My boss, Gloria, would have wanted me to call, but I wasn't going to wake her up. She slept little enough as it was. I would go home, turn the notes I was taking into a report, and then get some rest. Tomorrow was the weekly CAP-C Community Initiative board meeting; I could give my report to everyone then.

I was so intent on keying in my notes that I didn't look up as I rounded the corner toward the elevator. I just caught a glimpse of movement out of the corner of my eye, and then I was jerked backwards.

A hand came down over my mouth, stopping me as I pulled in breath to scream. The smell of him—sharp and dangerous—filled my nose and mouth and made my head spin.

Nevala.

I started to twist away, but he shoved me into an empty hospital room and kicked the door shut behind us. He kept one hand over my mouth and wrapped the other around my arms, pulling me up against him so that my back touched his chest. My shoulders tightened and I felt the shift trying to take over again.

"Be still," he hissed into my ear. His breath fluttered against my neck and my heart pounded in response. "You can't be seen here."

What does that mean?

I stopped struggling and nodded warily.

He lifted his arms away and the air rushed in, cool where his hands had been hot against me.

I turned to face him, backing up until my knees hit the hospital bed behind me. I didn't say anything; I still hadn't decided whether or not to run screaming. But he was between me and the door. I would have to get past him first.

Nevala and I stared at one another, the sound of our breathing harsh.

The doctor finally broke the silence. "You're not possible," he said, running one hand through his hair as he shook his head.

I ignored the implications of the statement. "Counselors? Yes, we are."

He gave me a sharp look. "That's not what I meant." He took a step forward. I leaned farther back, but I was trapped—I would either have to climb up on the bed or push my way past him. I wasn't sure which would be better.

Then it was too late—he grabbed my upper arms and stared into my eyes. His hands burned hot against my skin. His eyes, too, glittered feverishly, golden highlights churning through the brown.

The intensity of his stare captured me. I drew in another breath, full of the scent of him, and my head swam. The color leached out of the room. This time, though, I couldn't look away from him, couldn't hide the way my eyes changed, the pupils narrowing and lengthening. The room shifted into shades of gray, and his golden eyes turned silvery as they held my own.

He inhaled sharply as he saw the transformation and his hands tightened convulsively.

"How are you here?" he whispered, shaking his head.

He pulled me closer to him, staring into my eyes. My

pulse pounded in my temples. The muscles of my abdomen started to roil; I was about to shift, and I couldn't control it.

And I might just be okay with that, some quiet, still part of my mind whispered from far away, *because this man terrifies me. I might have a better chance against him in my serpent form.*

But something—some instinct deeper than thought—urged me to maintain my humanity.

I still couldn't break eye contact; his gaze was hypnotic.

He leaned in and kissed me.

THREE

I'm not the kind of woman who goes around kissing strange men—especially ones with hypnotic gold eyes who set off every internal warning system I've got.

And as a general rule, I avoid making out with men who drag me into dark rooms against my will.

But all those rules went out the window when this man kissed me.

His lips burned against mine, searing something deep inside, heating me to my core.

The almost peppery scent that had frozen me earlier now flooded my senses. His hands dropped from my shoulders and ran down my arms, wrapping around my waist and pulling me closer to him.

Muscles that moments ago had been writhing in an attempt to shapeshift now twisted to move closer to him.

He leaned me backwards and the edge of the bed pushed against the back of my knees. He moaned against my mouth and my knees started to go weak. He ran one hand down past the side of my waist and pulled one leg up, wrapping it around him. I could feel him against me, heat pouring through his body and into mine.

We leaned further over the bed.

Through the heat sliding into me from him, I heard the faint sound of a voice from the hospital PA system. The sound penetrated, shocking me back into myself.

I pushed back from him and rotated out of his arms, ducking under them to walk backwards toward the door. He spun to face me, and we stared at each other, still breathing heavily.

"What the hell was that?" I brushed my sleeves down over my arms and straightened my shirt. *When had it started to drift up over my waist?*

Nevala watched my hands, his eyes still swirling with golden intensity.

I took a step back. "Answer me, or I'm going to report you to the hospital for assault."

"You won't do that." He sounded confident.

"You don't want anyone here knowing about you."

My heart stuttered and my arms and legs went numb. "What do you mean?"

He smiled wider, and this time I saw that his canine teeth were a little elongated and far too sharp. "You don't want anyone to know you're a shapeshifter."

It was the first time anyone other than my parents had said the word. I took a deep breath to call his bluff, but his next words left me frozen in place.

"Because if anyone here knew what you were," he said, "they'd want me to do my duty. And technically, my job is to kill you."

And that was it: the moment I lost my already-tenuous grasp on my identity as a human as my animal instincts took over. The world grayed out, tiny flecks of light sparking inside what I'd always considered a cloud of magic surrounding me.

Shifting doesn't hurt, precisely, but it's not a comfortable experience, either—bones and muscles pop and grind as they compress and stretch, reforming themselves into a new shape. And there's always a moment of heart-stopping panic between the realization that I've lost my limbs and the acceptance of my serpentine body.

The whole process takes less than a minute, but it's a minute of vulnerability, and I always come out of it prepared to strike.

I don't know if that part's instinct, or maybe some sort of early training.

I remember waking up in Dad's herpetology lab that first morning. Everything before that is a blank. Dad and I have speculated that I underwent some kind of trauma. After all, something had happened to leave me stranded out in the West Texas desert where he found me, alone, all those years ago.

In any case, this shift was no exception. As the mist cleared from my eyes, I found myself reared back, hood fully extended, prepared to strike.

But Dr. Nevala sat perfectly still, simply watching me with those eyes of his—though through my shifted eyes, they looked silver rather than golden.

Weaving back and forth, prepared to move quickly if necessary, I held his gaze.

A slow, breathy sigh half-whistled from his lips. "Wow," he said, speaking quietly. "Your animal form is as beautiful as your human one."

I hissed, in part to illustrate my disdain for his appraisal, but also to taste the air surrounding us.

He wasn't lying—I could scent his admiration, sparkling across my vomeronasal organ. The flavor of his tone was much like my father's when he worked with his own snakes.

This was not a man who feared snakes.

I looped the lower part of my body out of my clothing, now puddled on the floor beneath me. Then I slid sideways to the cool tile floor, never taking my gaze off the human man in front of me.

In this form, the heat that poured from his burned against my skin even more intensely, and I found myself wanting to coil around him, soak up some of that warmth for myself.

You can't snuggle up to a man who just threatened to kill you, Lindi.

But I could appreciate how hot he ran.

"Ms. Parker," the doctor said. "I don't think you can make your way out of the hospital alone—not without being seen."

He was right. I hadn't really thought this through. Even if I did make it out of the hospital without being seen, I would end up at my car. I kept an extra key hidden in a wheel-well for just this kind of emergency, along with a set of clothes in the trunk, so I would be able to shift into my human form and drive away—but only after I spent several long, naked minutes illuminated by the bright streetlight I'd parked under for safety's sake.

Note to self: park in dark corners from now on.

Nevala had been watching me as I processed all of these ideas. I don't know how he knew when I reached the logical conclusion, but he said, "I'm going to step out of the room. I'll stand outside and keep anyone else from coming in until you tell me otherwise. Okay?"

I dipped my head once to let him know his plan worked for me, but I still watched the doctor carefully as he skirted around me, hugging the walls. I didn't taste any fear in the air, though, so keeping his distance might have been for my benefit.

At the door, he stopped and looked back. "But we are going to have to talk, Ms. Parker. I don't think you have any idea how much trouble you could be in."

I didn't acknowledge that statement, torn between a desperate desire to learn something—anything—about my origins, and an equally strong determination to stay away from someone who suggested that his community expected him to murder me.

When the door swung shut behind him, I began the process of moving back into my human shape. The shift took longer this time. Repeated shifting over short periods of time uses up much more energy than it does if I give myself time to recover.

Panicked shifting is also an energy-suck.

In any case, I struggled back into my clothes and pulled my hair into a loose knot at the nape of my neck.

I knocked lightly on the door from the inside and said, "Dr. Nevala?" in the most neutral tone I could as I pushed it open.

But Nevala was gone. In his place stood a stone-faced security guard, who nodded at me. "Ma'am. The doctor said I was to see you safely to your vehicle." Everything about his body language—from the 'parade rest' stance with his hands loosely clasped in front of him and his back ramrod straight, to the overly grim look on his face— suggested that he was determined to take this job seriously. I wondered briefly if Nevala had put a bug up his ass about keeping me safe, or if this was the guy's normal demeanor.

In any case, I didn't try to convince him that I could walk alone. Nevala's conversation had rattled me, and I found myself glancing around to make sure I wasn't ambushed by those other shifters—the ones who would expect Nevala to 'do his duty' and kill me.

Assuming he knows what he's talking about.

Assuming he isn't flat-out insane.

At the car, I turned to dismiss the guard, only to find him holding out a folded piece of paper. "The doctor said to give this to you before you left," he intoned. I stared at it as if it were the snake, rather than me—and not the happy, loving, shape-shifting kind of snake, but a creepy, evil, poisonous, hanging-out-in-Eden kind.

But whatever the note contained, it wasn't the guard's fault, so I plucked it out of his hand and slid into my car. The guard was still watching me, so I dropped the note onto the passenger seat, as if I weren't half-desperate to read what it said.

As I pulled out of the parking lot, I began scanning the streets for somewhere to pull over and read what Nevala had sent.

But first, I wanted to put a little distance between me and the hospital full of shapeshifters who might want me dead.

I was halfway home before I realized that I had lost my phone somewhere in that hospital room.

CHAPTER
FOUR

I was late to work the next morning. I hadn't slept well, and that was after staying up an extra hour to compose and email a report to Gloria.

I had finally decided, after much tossing and turning, to try to ignore what had happened with Kade Nevala. Still, I couldn't help returning over and over again to the way my body had reacted to his touch. Responding so eagerly to his kiss had been an aberration on my part, and I was going to assume that the doctor was having some sort of mental breakdown. My other option—the one that, as a counselor, I knew I should take, was to report him to the hospital.

The idea of reporting him made me anxious, though. If I had understood Emma correctly, then the hospital worked with other shapeshifters. And Nevala had said I wasn't possible; I could only assume that he knew what I was even before I shifted. If he had any doubts, they had been erased.

I didn't drift off to sleep until the sky outside my window began to lighten.

I was still mostly asleep when my home phone rang. I

didn't use it often, preferring my cell, but I kept it in case cell service went out and someone needed to reach me.

"Morning, sunshine," my boss Gloria sang out.

"You got my report, right?" My voice was blurry.

"Yep. Printed, signed, and filed. But the DA has called a special meeting about a new case. All hands on deck. I've got coffee brewing, so put on your happy face and come on in. You've got ninety minutes." She was far too cheerful, but the idea of a new case piqued my interest. I needed something to turn off the repeating clip of last night running through my head.

"Any idea what's up?" I asked.

"Nope. The quicker you get here, the sooner we'll find out. So hurry up."

Without new-case details to distract me, I continued to obsess about Nevala and his revelations all the way through taking a quick shower, pulling on a business-like skirt and blouse, giving my face the barest dusting of powder and lip gloss, and driving to work.

The last thing I wanted was anyone else knowing about me. I worked hard to ignore my animal side. I shifted as rarely as possible—although I could shift whenever I wanted to, I had learned to keep it down to about once a month. At that point, I had to find a time and a place to let that side of me free. It wasn't connected with the moon or anything, but if I didn't shift on my own, my body would do it without my consent. I had gone out to my parents' ranch just two weeks earlier and spent the day sunning my snake-self on a rock. I shouldn't have to change again for another two weeks.

The fact that I had shifted last night worried me.

Hell. Everything that had happened last night worried me.

Would Kade Nevala keep my secret? Could I trust him

not to tell other shapeshifters about me? Should I try to find out more about them? About him?

No. I would just ignore the entire situation. I pulled into a spot in the almost-full parking lot of the CAP-C and checked my makeup in the mirror.

No one else could know what I was.

It was safer that way.

I was safer.

I swung out of the car and walked into the building, feeling better than I had since I'd left the hospital the previous night.

Until I walked into the boardroom and came face-to-face with Dr. Kade Nevala himself.

I stumbled to a stop and took a step toward the door, but backed into Detective Moreland, who was just coming in.

"Careful, Lindi," Moreland said, steadying me with one hand while he held his coffee cup up high with the other.

"Oh. Sorry," I mumbled, still plotting to make my escape.

"You remember Dr. Nevala from the hospital last night?" Moreland asked, his voice genial.

Dammit. There goes my chance to leave unnoticed.

I stared hard at Nevala. "I remember."

"Please," Nevala said. "Call me Kade." He stuck out his hand and smiled, a twinkle in his golden eyes. I hesitated, but realized that several of the other people in the room were watching. I reached out to shake his hand. My fingers had gone icy cold—or maybe they just felt that way compared to the burning heat of his own.

"Hi," I murmured, retrieving my hand as quickly as possible. I moved around the conference table toward Gloria, as if I needed to speak to her. In fact, I did need to talk to her, had been planning to do so when I walked in the room, but at that moment I couldn't for the life of me remember why.

My boss looked up from some papers she was riffling through. "Oh, good. Lindi's here. We can get started." There was a murmur as everyone shuffled to seats. I took one about halfway down the table from Gloria and was irritated, but not entirely surprised, when Nevala ... Kade ... moved to sit next to me. A moment later he leaned forward and surreptitiously slipped my phone into my lap. I looked away from him.

"Hi, everyone," Gloria said. "First of all, I want to introduce our new board member, Dr. Kade Nevala." He waved from his seat. "Dr. Nevala has graciously offered to act as our medical specialist. He's a pediatrician at Kindred Hospital and is already working with Lindi on last night's case."

I clenched my teeth. He wouldn't be working on any other cases if I had my way.

"Okay. Lindi and Daniel, bring us up to speed on the Camelli case before we get to the new stuff?" Gloria leaned forward with her elbows on the table and looked at us expectantly.

I let Moreland talk first. The board members listened carefully. The local District Attorney, Jason Barker, and his investigator, Scott Carson, took notes. By the time Moreland was done giving the basics of the case, I was calm enough to speak—as long as I didn't look in Kade Nevala's direction.

"I believe Emma Camelli," I said. "I think she was being abused. She openly admits to having killed her father—"

"Stepfather," Nevala interrupted.

"Stepfather," I said. "Okay. Stepfather. Even more likely, then."

"We'll have the rape kit back soon?" Gloria looked at

Nevala for confirmation, then continued when he nodded. "In the meantime, we'll schedule her for counseling sessions here. Jason? Scott? Where will she be?"

"She's in the hospital through tonight," Scott said, glancing down at his notes. "We'll get her moved through family court tomorrow, see if we can get her placed."

"She can't stay with her mother?" Nevala asked quietly.

"Not usually," the DA said. "In most cases, we'll keep her in custody until we can have her fully evaluated."

"I know the family," Nevala said in his calm voice. "I would argue for them to stay together. I know the mother would get a hotel room for them, if you want them out of the house during the investigation."

The DA paused, then said, "Fine. Works for me. Lindi, you'll get the information on where they land?"

"Sure," I said, making a note.

On good days, I know that the work we do is important. The children who come to us are damaged, in pain, needing solace and closure and often justice. The CAP-C board coordinated all of those things and even when the children's stories broke my heart, I knew that they were better off because our program existed. It was important to me to be part of this team, to work at carefully evaluating the cases that came to us.

Today, however, I couldn't concentrate. Next to me, Dr. Kade Nevala radiated heat, and I had an irrational desire to move closer to that warmth.

I resisted the urge, refocusing on the conversation at the table and trying to take notes on the cases we discussed.

"And that brings us to the new case," Gloria said, gesturing toward the DA and his investigator.

Jason stood up, smoothing his expensive tie down over his shirtfront as he got ready to speak. "Hi, all. Thanks for coming in on such short notice." He nodded to me, then to

Kade. At the DA's gesture, Scott turned off the lights and hit a button on his laptop to start a PowerPoint projection. A red case-file number appeared on the screen at the far end of the room.

"Before I pull up the images, I need to warn you: this is as bad as anything we've dealt with here. Worse." Jason's eyes flickered around the room, as if gauging whether or not we were prepared.

Images from Emma's room the night before flashed through my mind.

It couldn't be worse than that.

I was wrong.

Scott clicked a button, and the case number slid away, replaced by another picture.

It took my mind a few moments to parse the image on the screen. It looked like a broken doll, floating in a child's wading pool.

Jason's voice drifted over the horrific image. "This is Candice Blake, eight years old. She was found in her family's above-ground pool. Her arms and legs had been broken, and she couldn't get out of the pool before she drowned."

Click.

Several people gasped in the dark.

"Jenna Pack. A seven-year-old, kidnapped from her back yard. Some kids playing discovered her body two miles away in a wooded area. As you can see, she had been dismembered."

Click.

"Tasha Williams. Ten. Found hanging from a tree outside her home. Looked like a suicide until the medical examiner found signs of rape."

Click.

"Laura McCoy. Eleven. Disappeared walking home from

a friend's house last night. Found two hours later, shot through the head, execution-style."

Click.

"And last night, Charlotte Johnson, eight, was discovered strangled in a dry creek bed behind her house. "

God. All these poor little girls.

Tears pooled in my eyes, and I closed them to shut out the images.

I had become a counselor to help protect children. Living children, not dead ones. We worked with survivors at the CAP-C. I didn't know what I could possibly do to help with actual murder cases. I opened my mouth to ask, but Jason continued speaking. "Initially, there was no apparent connection among them. Different neighborhoods, schools, everything." Once again, he gestured at Scott, and the investigator turned the lights back on. We all blinked a little, trying not to make eye contact in the wake of such horrific visuals.

"In the course of our investigation," Jason said, "we discovered that the victims had two things in common. First, they all had siblings who had been counseled at the CAP-C for one reason or another."

"Oh, no," Gloria breathed from her chair at the end of the table, fisting her hands on the table.

"Second, they were all patients of Dr. Nevala's." With Jason's words, I flashed a glance at the man sitting next to me.

Kade's patients?

Did that mean that they were shapeshifters?

If so, I couldn't tell anyone.

Still ... maybe three things in common.

FIVE

I f all of the victims had CAP-C clients as siblings ... I waved a little to catch Jason's attention. "Does that mean that we're suspects or something?"

With an abbreviated shake of his head, Jason said, "No. We'll clear each of you individually, of course, but I'm confident that will happen quickly. Scott will get some information from each of you. But the main reason we've brought this to the CAP-C is that we want help sorting through your files to identify any other potential victims."

Gloria chewed on her bottom lip, tilting her blonde head to one side as she regarded Jason through narrowed eyes. "You know there might be confidentiality issues," she said.

"That's why I'm asking CAP-C to work with me on this," Jason replied. He glanced at me. "Lindi and Dr. Nevala were at the hospital with Emma Camelli last night, when the fourth murder was committed, so barring any new evidence, I'm assuming they're both clear."

"Gee, thanks," I muttered. The DA smiled at me tiredly.

"So do you really think these murders are connected?" I asked.

Moreland leaned over to see me past Nevala. "That's what we're hoping to find out, now that Dr. Nevala brought the connection to our attention."

This wasn't something that Scott had dug up, then. Or the police.

Speaking of . . . "Why aren't your guys handling this?" I asked Moreland.

"We're looking into a number of possibilities," the detective responded. "But cases involving children are especially delicate, and since the CAP-C grant allows for collaboration between agencies, we're taking advantage of some extra eyes on the cases. Especially since they're eyes with confidentiality clauses already in place." A tiny smile flashed across his face, acknowledging the pragmatic element of co-opting CAP-C personnel for the grunt work of digging through files.

Gloria, who had been jotting notes down on the legal pad in front of her, dropped her pen down onto the table and sat up a little straighter, her curly blonde hair bouncing a little with the motion. As usual, she looked like a former beauty-queen, moved into a soft, kindly middle-age. People often made the mistake of assuming she was as sweet as she appeared. Those people often paid for their mistake when she unleashed her sharp, analytical mind on them, via her equally incisive tongue.

Our secretary, Jose, called her "a needle in a cotton ball."

I might be the snake, but when it came to protecting children, Gloria was a viper.

I could see the calculation behind her eyes now. "Lindi, you and Kade spend today hitting the records, see what you can dig up. Start with these girls, since there won't be any confidentiality issues. Then move to the others." She turned to the DA. "Who's coordinating?"

Jason tilted his chin toward his investigator and responded to the table at large. "Scott's got everything. If you find anything at all suspicious, let him know and he'll pull together any necessary warrants to ferret out the rest."

"Your hospital agreed to let us dig through your patient records?" I asked the doctor.

Kade shrugged. "Not precisely."

"Can't you get in trouble for that? Because of HIPAA or something?"

"That's why Gloria made me a CAP-C board member—I signed all the nondisclosure and confidentiality paperwork that allows me to see your clients' records." With a nod, he hefted the strap of a soft leather bag he carried over his shoulder. "And you're not going to see any medical records that aren't already part of your files."

"That makes you the only person who knows everything about this case?"

"Until we get enough for a warrant, yes."

The setup made me uncomfortable—the limited flow of information was bad enough. The fact that everything we knew was coming through the man—the creature—who had all but assaulted me the night before caused my stomach to clench.

"How are we going to do this?" I asked. There had to be some way for me to verify any claims he made.

Why had Gloria trusted him so immediately?

Had he used some sort of weird enchantment on her? Did magic even exist?

I was about to spend hours working with someone who might be my sworn enemy, and I didn't have a clue about his abilities.

For that matter, I didn't know much about my own

abilities. My parents had taught me to be as human as possible.

I didn't know a damn thing about being a shapeshifter.

Somehow, I was going to have to find a way to get Dr. Kade Nevala alone to quiz him.

But first, we needed to find a killer.

"I know it's a tenuous connection, but it's all we've got. We need to find a way to identify possible future victims." Now that I was looking for it, I saw stress-lines around Jason's eyes and mouth.

"So what can we do?" I asked, suddenly more willing to cut the man some slack. He nodded his thanks to me.

"Scott's going to interview everyone else here so we can get you all officially cleared. In the meantime, I want Lindi and Dr. Nevala to compare notes on the victims." He shook his head and held up a hand, cutting off Gloria as she opened her mouth to speak. "Confidentiality doesn't survive death, Gloria. I just want to know if there's anything in the CAP-C files or the girls' medical records that might point us in the right direction."

Anxious to quiz Kade about shapeshifters, I gathered up the notebook I'd placed on the conference table in front of me. I hadn't taken any notes—quickly, I jotted down the four victims' names. As if I would forget them. "Anything else we need to know before we get started?"

"I'd rather not contaminate your observations. But we'll keep in touch," Jason said. "You and Dr. Nevala should trade numbers, too—you'll need to consult.

Dammit.

I felt Kade beside me, the heat pouring off of him reminding me of his hands against my skin, his lips slanted across mine.

When the meeting broke up, I headed toward the door, hoping to escape to my office, even for a moment.

Nevala followed me out. I stopped in the hall and faced him.

"What are you doing here?" I hissed.

One corner of his mouth crooked up in a half-smile. "Returning your phone?"

"That's not what I meant." I clamped my mouth shut as Scott passed us. He slowed, staring at me curiously.

"Everything okay, Lindi?" he asked.

"Fine," I said, but my voice shook.

Scott looked back and forth between me and Nevala. "Lunch today?" he finally asked.

"Sure," I said.

He moved on, but glanced back at us. Nevala continued to grin.

"My office. Now," I said, my voice tight. Spinning away from him, I marched down the hall without watching to see if he followed me.

When we reached my office, I shut the door and moved around to keep my desk between us. I have two wing-back chairs that I use to talk to clients, but they're set up to eliminate distance. I wanted to keep as much space between us as possible.

Kade looked around the office curiously. I had shelves of toy bins, books, art supplies. Anything that might help a child relax and play, and maybe even talk to me.

"This is nice," he said, nodding.

"I don't care what you think of my office," I said. "I want to know why you're here."

His mouth quirked up in that odd grin again. "Because I'm supposed to kill you."

CHAPTER
SIX

People don't like snakes. I actually get that—there's something viscerally appalling about an animal so different from oneself, made of muscle and scale rather than skin and bone. Snakes aren't fuzzy or cuddly or cute.

Not that I feel that way, of course. I love spending time in Dad's herpetarium, the small outbuilding that had formerly served the old house as a garage and now housed Dad's entire collection. When I'm there, I can close my eyes and listen to the gentle swish of scales over sand, the slight hiss of my brethren—or at least distant cousins—testing the air around them. I find it soothing.

As a child, I used to like to shift in the herpetarium and sun myself under the heat lamps. I couldn't often shift and go out into the real sun, because, Dad said, I had a dark secret to keep, and people would want to lock me up, study me, keep me caged for the rest of my life. The herpetarium was a nice alternative.

But I'm basically an okay person. I give loose change to homeless people, volunteer in a food bank, work to give hurt children a voice. My entire life has been about developing my human side—the side of me that is kind of cuddly and cute.

I hadn't ever imagined that my mere existence would be cause for someone to hunt me down and kill me in cold blood. So to speak.

I blinked hard and shook my head, hoping to dispel the sense of unreality that had been fogging my thinking since Emma had told me she *changed* her hand.

"Why would anyone want you to kill me?" I asked. "I've never hurt anyone."

"You shouldn't have come to the hospital last night," Nevala said. "It's dangerous for someone like you."

"You can't kill me. That's insane." A moment ago, all I had wanted was to get into my office. Now all I wanted was out.

"Wait," he said. "I can explain."

"No, you can't. You're a crazy man who assaulted me and then threatened me." Reaching behind me with one hand, I felt around for the door.

Nevala crossed his arms over his chest and glared at me. "I didn't assault you."

The assertion brought me to an abrupt halt. "You dragged me into a dark room and kissed me."

"I was checking to see what you were." His eyes flicked away from mine as he spoke.

Liar.

"Oh, really?" I squinted at him, hoping to see a telltale flush creep up his neck, but I couldn't tell if he was blushing —neither the ambient light in my office nor his own dark complexion gave me much to go on.

He sighed, and I flinched at the movement.

"I'm sitting down," he said, holding his hands up in surrender and taking his own step backwards until he could drop to the nearest chair. "I wouldn't do anything to hurt you. Please, let me explain." He focused those intense eyes on me, their hypnotic gold flecks holding me prisoner —almost as much as my own desire to learn what he thought I was.

Because God knows, I have no idea.

"And what you learned told you that you're supposed to kill me?" I finally asked.

"Supposed to," he said. "But I won't."

I had spent more time than I would ever admit to my adoptive parents searching for any indication of what I might be. I knew they would understand—but I think we were all afraid of what I might discover.

Like I was afraid now.

But Emma had known as soon as she'd seen me that I was a shapeshifter.

Nevala seemed to know more about me than I knew about myself.

Crap. I was going to have to hear the crazy man out.

"Okay," I said, pulling my hand away from the door and taking a half-step back into the room. "You have three minutes. Talk."

HE STARTED OVER. "You shouldn't have come to Kindred last night."

I took a deep breath. Might as well call his bluff. "Emma Camelli says Kindred Hospital is where all the shapeshifters go. Why would I care if they knew I went there?"

"Because you're not like other shapeshifters."

"How so?"

His golden brown eyes started to glow. I realized I was leaning over my desk toward him, again almost hypnotized by those eyes. "You're supposed to be extinct." He paused for a long moment. "If the rest of the shapeshifters knew you were still alive, they would expect me to take you down."

My hands started to shake as the bitter taste of adrenaline flooded my mouth. "Still alive?" I asked. My voice stayed steady, but from the way Kade's nostrils flared, I suspected he could smell the pre-shift chemicals surging through my body.

He closed his eyes, gathering his thoughts. "How much do you actually know about your past?"

A short bark of laughter escaped me. "Nothing. Not a damn thing."

"Then how did you end up at Kindred?"

"I told you. I was on call the night Emma Pack killed her father. She and her mother insisted we take her to your hospital." I gestured widely, taking in the whole building. "That's it."

Kade's whistle was low. "Holy shit. So you really just happened to end up there?"

Tension coiled in my chest, getting ready to burst out in a full-blown snake-shift if I didn't get information right now. "Will you please quit quizzing me and tell me what it is that you know?" I tried to push the questions down, but they popped out faster than he could possibly answer them. "Do you know who my parents are? Are they still alive? Why did they abandon me? Who am I?" The last question came out on something of a wail, and I slapped my own hand over my mouth to stop myself from continuing to speak—or possibly cry.

Kade blinked his golden eyes in surprise. "You really don't know?"

Clenching my teeth against further exclamations, I gritted out, "Tell me what I am."

"You're a lamia," he said.

"That's a snake shifter?" I thought I had dealt with all of my abandonment issues in my training to become a counselor—in order to gain my license, I had to go through hours and hours of therapy myself, both to learn the techniques and so my professors and mentors could be sure I wasn't too messed up myself to work with others.

I had never tried to hide the fact that I had been adopted as a child—just that the parents who abandoned me had been able to turn into snakes. That kind of claim can get you banned from working with anyone at all, at least as a professional counselor.

Despite the hours of counseling, though, I apparently still had deep reserves of abandonment issues, because instead of asking Kade, "What else do you know?" I burst into tears.

Some part of me expected Kade to move into his professional persona—don't pediatricians have to deal with weepy patients on a fairly regular basis?—but his ability to deal with sobbing weresnakes apparently matched mine to stay as cool and calm as I had intended during this encounter. He stared at me, open-mouthed, then managed to pat me on the shoulder.

It took a few moments, but I finally pulled myself together enough to speak again. "Tell me everything."

Kade nodded, and drew in a deep breath.

"Like I said, you're a lamia, and traditionally, it would be my job to kill you."

"You've said that already," I noted.

"Yeah, but it seemed like a good idea to go back to the beginning." A slight smile quirked up the corner of Kade's mouth. "I wasn't entirely sure you'd heard all of that last bit."

I narrowed my eyes at him. "If it's your job to kill me, then what are you?"

"I'm a ..." Kade paused, chewing on his bottom lip a bit, then shook his head. "Might as well say it. I'm a mongoose shifter."

"A what?" My tone almost conveyed the disbelief I felt.

He held his hands up in front of him as if shielding himself from my potential ridicule. "I know. It sounds stupid. But if you think about it, it's no stranger than a snake shifter."

Suddenly, I flashed back on Jason saying we would have to "ferret out the information," and it made me want to giggle. *Or mongoose out the rest, anyway.*

I considered the possibilities for a moment. "So if there are were-snakes and ..." I paused, shaking my head. "And were-mongooses ... mongeese? Anyway, if you and I exist, then ..."

"Then what other types of shifters are there?" Kade crooked one eyebrow up at me, and I nodded rapidly, just in case the expression meant he was about to turn the potential for ridicule around on me. He shrugged. "Just about any kind you can think of, probably. I don't know all of them, though we get our fair share through here."

I hazarded a guess. "Werewolves?"

"Oh, yeah. Probably more of them than anything else, though not as many here as in other parts of the country, I understand." He began ticking them off on his fingers. "And the other major predators—various big cats, like lions and tigers."

I couldn't stop myself. "And bears?"

He blew out a sigh, but he grinned as he said, "Yes. And bears. But others, too—mostly mammals, like raccoons and badgers. More rabbits than you'll ever realize. They're good at hiding."

I could tell he was skirting around something that was going to be unpleasant, so I prodded him. "And non-mammals?"

"Fewer of them—I suspect it's from a basic incompatibility of human and non-mammalian systems, though I'm not certain."

Letting myself get sidetracked for a moment, I asked, "Aren't you their doctor? Shouldn't you know things like that?"

"Probably. But until recently, the elders just called it magic and left it at that. There was no such thing as shifter science until the last few decades." His lips twisted wryly. "And the truce among the shifter species is even more recent than that—so even if we wanted to study the shifter mechanism, we could only study our own kind." He paused. "Or the bodies of the enemies we killed."

"Like lamia?" I asked.

"Exactly." He leaned over and brushed his fingertip against the tops of my fingers. At some point during the conversation, I had interlaced them tightly without noticing. Now a shiver ran up my arm and down my spine at his touch.

I couldn't tell if he was trying to distract me or comfort me. Or maybe something else altogether.

More to the point, I couldn't tell what I wanted him to do.

I chose to ignore it. "So if there's some huge shapeshifter truce, why would everyone still want you to kill me?"

"Because," he said, "the lamia were the last of the shifters to hold out on the truce. Until a little over twenty years ago, they were still hunting down and killing other shapeshifters." He quit stroking my hand and leaned back in the chair. "It's as true in the shifter world as it is in the human world."

I nodded. "Snakes are feared and misunderstood. That's what my father always says, anyway." At Kade's look of surprise, I corrected myself. "My adoptive father."

"Well," Kade said, "they're feared, anyway."

I rubbed my hands across my eyes. "None of this tells me anything about what you're doing here, right now, in my office."

The grin that had been playing around his lips since he'd entered the room finally dropped off his face. "Seriously, I'm here to help figure out how to protect those kids."

I stared at him for a long, silent moment. "Okay," I finally said, matching his own serious tone. "If you mean it, then let's get started."

SEVEN

An hour and half later, I was ready to pull my hair out.

It had taken us at least thirty minutes of that time to figure out how to cross-reference the materials that I wasn't allowed to look at with the CAP-C files. After far too much negotiating, we had finally arranged a system: I read off names, he checked them against his list, and we either moved on or flagged the file for a more detailed examination later. The whole comedy-of-errors process wasn't helped by the fact that being trapped in a room with Dr. Mongoose only heightened my awareness of him. Combined with the memory of the kiss the night before, it was a wonder I didn't crawl out of my own skin.

Literally.

Every time he leaned over to take a file from me, his spicy scent washed across me on a wave of body heat that sent chills racing across me, bringing my nipples to attention and tightening the muscles of my back until I wanted to coil around him, writhing closer and closer to the core of that warmth.

It wasn't merely sexual attraction. I had felt that before. While lust was obviously a component of this strange compulsion to touch him, there was more to it. Something primal, and dangerous.

From the way the golden highlights in his eyes sparked whenever our gazes met, he felt it, too.

But neither of us mentioned it.

I didn't bring up any of my questions about shifters, either. Hoping to keep this meeting more professional than the last time we had been shut in a room together, I left the file-room door open so that anyone walking down the hall could see us. Although it kept the sexual tension down to a dark simmer, it kept me from quizzing him, as well.

Worse, we hadn't found anything useful yet. No CAP-C clients who were also Kade's patients. No siblings, either.

Granted, we were only partway through the client list. But it had been tedious, frustrating work.

So when Scott stuck his head in through the door a little before noon, I was pathetically grateful for the reprieve. "Ready for lunch?" the DA's investigator asked me.

"God, yes." I stood up from my chair and stretched my back.

Snagging my purse from the back of my chair, I turned to Kade. "I'll meet you back here around 1:30, okay?" Without waiting for an answer, I tucked my arm in Scott's and tugged him down the hall toward the lobby.

I'd known Scott Carson for about a year. He joined the DA's office six months after I started working for the CAP-C, and we'd been paired on a few cases. What had started out as a necessity—grabbing something to eat on the way to interview a child—had turned into a ritual. We had lunch together whenever he was in the building, at least once a week.

He was interested in something more, I suspected. I

could smell it on him—the hint of desire and anxiety that human men exuded as they geared up to ask me out. The fact that he hadn't worked around to it yet was a bit of a surprise.

I couldn't decide if I was disappointed, or glad. Something about him bothered me, though I'd never been able to pin down exactly what it was.

Maybe it was just that human relationships were a problem for me.

Not the basics. I had companions, friends, even lovers.

But inevitably, I kept some distance in those relationships. I had yet to meet anyone I trusted enough to tell my shapeshifter secret.

And even if I wanted to share that information at some point, it led to a whole host of other concerns. I didn't even know, for example, if I could have children with a human male.

Or if I should, even if it were possible.

Yet another reason to find a way to corner Kade Nevala and force him to answer my questions.

For now, though, I would simply enjoy Scott's company.

As we reached the building entrance, a wave of hostility thudded against my back and I stumbled. Scott, still holding my arm, caught me up against him. "You okay?" Nothing but concern showed in his voice, but as I leaned against him, I licked my lips, and I could taste his physical reaction in the air around me. Glancing over my shoulder, I saw Kade standing at the end of the hallway, arms crossed as he scowled at me. Again I was struck by his sheer physical presence. Scott was physically bigger, but everything about Kade radiated power.

Right now, he also oozed anger—the remains of that animosity that had hit me with such force moments before.

"I'm fine," I muttered, but I threw a quelling look at Kade.

It did nothing to quash his antagonism, if the continuing waves of heated spice pouring off of him were anything to go on.

As if kissing me once—against my will—gave him any right to be angry when I went to lunch with someone else.

We were seriously going to have to have a talk about that alpha-male bullshit. Alpha-mongoose.

Whatever the hell it was.

In any case, I planned to ignore it for the moment, despite the surge of rage that followed me out the door.

LUNCH REMINDED me why I enjoyed Scott's company so much. His straightforward conversation and easy laugh soothed me—and after a morning spent in the company of The Brooding Mongoose, I needed that.

"So what's up with Nevala?" Scott asked as we strolled into our favorite Mexican restaurant in downtown Fort Worth. "He seemed fine this morning, but when we left, I sensed some tension."

Wow. If Scott could feel it, then I knew it was rough. I was used to being attuned to human emotions, sometimes even more than the individuals experiencing them.

My ability to sense what the people around me were feeling made me a better counselor in some ways.

In other ways, it was a problem. My snake half sometimes prompted me to strike out when I sensed weakness.

It was a trait my parents had worked with me to overcome, and part of why Dad had steered me toward working with children.

"I'm not sure," I hedged. "Have you worked with him before?"

Scott shook his head. "I think he's pretty new to the area. Not that we work with Kindred Hospital much, anyway."

"Not our clientele," I agreed. In oh, so many ways. Kindred had a reputation of catering to wealthier patients. And apparently, to shiftier patients, as well. Most of CAP-C's clients were from families who either couldn't afford private counseling, or who needed short-term help while they arranged for something more permanent. Most of the cases that involved trips to hospitals—rape, physical abuse—came to us either through Brinks' Children's or the local emergency rooms.

"What do you think of these cases?" I asked once we were seated and the waitress had taken our orders.

"Off the record?" Scott grabbed a tortilla chip and dunked it in his tiny salsa cup. Crunching into it, he stared off into the distance, his green eyes narrowed. I waited, used to his thinking process. "I think they're connected, either through Kindred or CAP-C."

"And?" I dumped sugar into my iced tea, then dropped the lemon wedge from the edge of the glass into Scott's drink. He nodded his thanks.

"We'll figure it out, eventually. Whatever the connection, it's not obvious. There's no other commonality, not in the method of killing or in the choice of victims. Hell, it wasn't even one case until Nevala brought it to us two days ago."

I froze. "Two days ago? Kade has known for two days that he was going to be working with us?"

"Well, one day. Jason called him yesterday afternoon."

Kade had known I worked for the CAP-C. Why the hell hadn't he said anything?

The waitress brought our plates, and Scott smiled at her. She flushed in pleasure, and I was reminded of how attractive Scott really was, with his sandy blond hair and his green eyes.

I was suddenly tempted to ask him out myself, but I couldn't tell if the urge came from an actual desire to go on a date with him, or some competitive desire to claim him before the waitress could.

Or maybe to show Kade Nevala that his anger didn't have any impact on me.

I tamped down the impulse.

Better review that one before acting on it.

I could almost hear Dad's voice. *Control, Lindi. Remember, you're in charge of you.*

Anyway, for all that I enjoyed Scott's company, something had always kept me from asking him out on a real date before.

I should probably pay attention to that instinct.

Control.

I was going to have a full afternoon, and who knew how long after, to practice maintaining control around Dr. Kade Nevala.

Might as well start now.

CHAPTER
EIGHT

M aybe I'm wrong. Maybe humans can smell emotions and intentions, at least sometimes. Because when Scott wheeled his big, black pickup into the CAP-C parking lot, he didn't shut it off immediately. Instead, he rested his forearms on the steering wheel and turned his head to face me. "I think we should do this some other time."

I pretended not to understand. "Scott, we go out to lunch all the time."

"I mean, some time that isn't lunch. I think we should go out." His intent gaze bored into mine. "Dinner, drinks, a movie."

"Like a date?" I kept my tone light, unsure of my real response.

"Not *like* a date. An actual date. This weekend. Friday?"

"Okay." I drew the word out, nodding. "But we take it very slowly from there."

He grinned. "You seem pretty sure there's going to be a 'from there.'"

"Don't be an ass." I opened the door and swung my legs

out, then glanced back at him over my shoulder. "You know you want a 'from there.'" I hopped down to the ground and sashayed to the door without looking back.

I was grinning as I stepped into my office to grab a mint and touch up my makeup, and I heard Scott whistling as he stopped to speak to Gloria, who had, as usual, chosen lunch at her desk. She had, in the past, joined us occasionally for lunch, but those instances grew rarer as her case-load picked up.

I had wondered more than once if her absence was one of her unsubtle attempts to get me to date more.

If so, it might be working.

Kade was already in the records room when I returned. I don't know if he ever even left for lunch.

"Enjoy your break?" he asked. His mild tone belied the sheer rage that still boiled off him. He radiated so much heat that it was almost too much to bear. I shifted away from him, and from his quick glance, he noticed the move.

"I always enjoy lunch with Scott." I worked to match his outward tone. Initially, I didn't address the emotional tenor of the discussion.

Hell, I didn't even understand the undertones at play here.

Kade continued flipping through manila file folders too quickly. I wasn't sure he could even read their labels, much less review the contents.

After a long pause, I decided to dive into the conversation I'd been avoiding all day.

As I stood up to shut the door, Kade's manic folder examinations slowed. I still tasted his anger fizzing through the air, but it slowed a little as curiosity threaded through it —a line of sharp inquiry, like lime in an over-carbonated soda.

I leaned against the door, my hands still on the doorknob behind me. "I don't know anything about...." Pausing, I listened to make sure no one was walking down the hall, flicked my tongue out against my lower lip to test the currents, make sure we were truly alone. Still, I wasn't willing to be specific, just in case someone overheard us. "About your world."

The sparks of anger filling the room subsided further as one corner of Kade's mouth twisted up. "The world of medicine?"

Okay. I could work with that. "Yeah. Sure. Medicine. The thing is, I don't know how ... doctors ... interact. I don't know the rules. And because I've never been around ... doctors ... I don't read them very well."

He dropped the folder he was holding into a stack in front of him and his hands finally stilled as he stared at me. After a long pause, he tilted his head. "You're not like any other ... counselor ... I've ever met, or even heard about. You defy everything I've ever been taught about your kind."

"And that makes you angry?"

"It confuses me." He paused, and his smile turned wry. "And being confused makes me angry."

I pushed away from the door without opening it again. "If we're really going to work together, I think maybe we should have a more detailed conversation. Somewhere safe. Not here, not Kindred."

Kade nodded. "My place?"

My heart thudded at the thought of being alone with him in his territory, and I couldn't tell if the reaction was terror or anticipation.

Maybe a little of both.

If he could hear my reaction, he gave no outward sign of it. But his scent darkened, and his temperature rose.

I imagined an infinite loop of reaction and response in the confined space of anyplace that could be called his, and

49

shuddered. "Someplace a little more public," I suggested. "Or at least outdoors."

"Agreed." He nodded.

"Sundance Square?" I suggested. "It would keep us from being overheard, I suspect. At least by anyone who knew us."

"I'm on duty at Kindred tomorrow and Thursday," he said. "How about Friday night?"

"Oh." I stuttered a little. "I can't. Not Friday. I have plans."

"So change them."

"Why don't you change your work schedule around?"

"That's not so easy for a doctor to do."

"And you think it's easy for me to just change my plans around entirely? That doesn't seem quite fair."

The air had begun sparking against my tongue again.

"And it's no good getting mad about it," I said. "I can have as much of a personal life as I want, even if it confuses and angers you."

"With humans?" he hissed. "With that investigator for the DA?"

"Is that such a bad thing, having a relationship with someone?" I counted off on my fingers. "He's smart, he's funny, he's attractive as hell."

That elicited an actual growl from the were-mongoose.

"Oh," I said. "Is that jealousy?"

"No," he snarled. "That's concern for the human." His voice rose at the end of his statement, and I put my hands up, palms out, to placate him.

"We need to put this conversation on hold," I said. "I'll see if I can change my plans for Friday. What's a good alternative day for you if I can't?"

The level of heat rolling off him dropped a tiny bit. "I could do Sunday." His arm twitched, and I glanced down at it just long enough to see a muscle contract, as if he were holding off a shift.

And God help me, I was glad to be able to elicit another reaction from him.

I wasn't entirely certain what that said about me. Maybe that my inner snake was currently winning the never-ending battle between compassion and a cold-blooded desire to win, to survive, to take down whatever prey I found.

It was a battle I fought on some level almost every day. Apparently today, my serpentine self wanted to watch Kade Nevala squirm.

I pushed that desire down, hard, along with the errant thought that my mammal side might be okay with some squirming, too.

This wasn't going to help us catch a serial killer, or save any children.

"Got your list ready?" I asked.

Kade nodded tersely, and I once again settled into the search for common patients and clients.

CHAPTER
NINE

At the end of the day, I needed comfort.

Kade and I hadn't had any real luck in our search, though we had about a morning's worth of files to go through the next day.

But all those children, in pain.

I had worked with most of them. One at a time, it was easy to take their pain, walk them through the issues that brought them to me—rape, incest, physical and emotional abuse. Horrors that no children should ever have to see.

Sometimes it made me think I shouldn't hope to have any children of my own. I wasn't even sure I could—I didn't know a damn thing about a shapeshifter's reproductive system. Would the shifting kill off any developing fetus? Or would it shift along with me?

For that matter, I didn't even know if I was an egg-laying snake or a viviparous snake who would give birth to live snakes. Both kinds exist in nature, but I didn't even know if I was natural—or some sort of freak of nature. Or maybe magical. Mystical.

Monstrous.

Anyway, I wasn't willing to test any theories through trial and error, so I had decided a long time ago that I would never have children of my own.

Instead, I helped save other people's hurt and abandoned children.

The unloved, unwanted, mistreated offspring of another race entirely.

The irony of a snake offering comfort to humans wasn't lost on me.

And after a whole day of reminders of the ways that people damaged one another, I wanted to be reminded that people could also be kind. Could love children who weren't even their own.

So I headed out to my parents' ranch.

When I pulled my Camry across the cattle guard laid over the culvert, the dust that flew up around me smelled like home.

Dad's truck was gone, so I swung through the house, calling out for Mom as I went. She wasn't home, either, but steaks marinating in a bowl on the counter suggested that they would be home for dinner.

I could wait. Television didn't sound appealing, though.

Late-afternoon sunlight slanted through the kitchen window, illuminating tiny dust-motes dancing in the air. Opening the back door, I surveyed the streaks of sunlight stretching across the porch.

Not warm enough.

Dad kept the herpetarium door unlocked most of the time, despite the fake rock that Mom had given him years ago to hide an extra key. He kept losing the extra key, too.

Today wasn't the first time I'd been glad of that fact.

The interior of the room was warm and dim, the heat lamps turned on in about half the terrariums.

Drawing in the slightly musty smells on deep breath, I

flicked out my tongue to take the emotional temperature of the room.

Nothing unusual had disrupted these snakes' lives recently.

If they could taste my disquiet, I had no sense of it.

I stopped by and spoke to a few of my favorites—Suzy, the albino python, in particular. When I was younger, I had thought I might be able to actually communicate with some of Dad's specimens.

Maybe I could.

Or maybe it had simply made me feel better to believe that these animals, too, were part of my heritage.

In any case, Suzy always seemed to exude a deep, abiding calm. An internal serenity completely different from anything humans had to offer.

I needed that today.

Unlike the previous night in the hospital, I had time to prepare for this shift. Locating the key to the shed on one of the top shelves (not an uncommon place for Dad to leave it), I set it out in its hiding place and flipped the bolt to the locked position. The locked door would let Dad know I was inside—he would knock before he unlocked it and came in, so I would be able to let him know if I hadn't shifted yet.

Removing the screen lid from Suzy's terrarium, I set it to the side and let my hand drift across her white and yellow body. She flicked her tongue out, then rubbed her head alongside my arm, the rest of her coils rippling out and over. Making space for me next to her.

Who says snakes don't have feelings?

Quickly, I stripped out of my clothes, folded them neatly, and set them on the floor next to the terrarium lid. I pressed my torso up against the glass outside Suzy's enclosure, leaning down into it just a little.

Then I shifted.

In the herpetarium, the moment of panic that came with losing arms and legs flickered, then disappeared, subsumed by the sense of belonging I always felt here.

For the first time ever, I wondered if shifting among my own kind would eliminate that feeling altogether.

As the world around me grayed out entirely, I flicked my tail up into the air and slid into Suzy's enclosure.

The python slid out of my way, making room for me inside the circle of light shed by the heat lamp.

With an internal sigh, I coiled as tightly as possible next to Suzy. She drew herself across the glass floor, rustling in the aspen bedding as she encircled me, drawn to the heat generated by the shift and remaining from my mammal form.

Or maybe because she realizes I need comfort?

I didn't know for sure, but I preferred the latter.

Once we were arranged, twisted together and resting, I let my mind rest, along with my body.

It was easier to do in this form.

Lamia form.

The thought drifted across my mind, then was gone, simply another piece of information to process—not consciously, but in my back-brain, along with the muted sounds of the other reptiles as they breathed and moved, the feeling of heat soaking in to my muscles from the lamp, the distant smell of the mice in the freezer that Dad would feed the snakes later in the week, the comforting touch of Suzy's length against me, the tastes that drifted across the Jacobson's organ in the top of my mouth, offering information that had no mammalian equivalent.

It was good to come home.

I don't know how much time had passed when Dad came into the herpetarium.

He walked straight to Suzy's terrarium. He knew me that well.

"Hey, sweetheart," he said, dropping his hand down to run a finger across the top of my head, then down my neck and along my spine. The muscles along my sides rippled in concert.

I don't know if full-blood snakes can love.

But I know that I do.

"Mom's in the house cooking if you want to shift and dress and join us for dinner." His voice came through muffled, as did all sounds, bouncing off the tiny cochlear bones in my head. The longer I stayed in serpentine form, the more difficult it would become to translate those sounds into words.

I don't know how long I had been living as a snake when Dad first found me, but when I first shifted, I couldn't speak—whether because I had never learned how, or because I had forgotten, we didn't know.

As a teenager, I had shifted in a fit of pique over some rule Mom and Dad had implemented and didn't shift back for two weeks. I had never told my parents, but my decreasing understanding of what they said to me had been my primary motivation for coming back into human form.

That, and the realization that I had almost stopped caring what they were saying to me.

If I hadn't had years of Dad's training in how to be a human, I don't know if I would have been able to come back to myself.

More clearly than words, though, I had always felt—smelled, tasted—my parents' intentions and emotions.

I liked to think that their love could draw me back from any edge.

As Dad withdrew and I pulled myself up to shift back to

my human form, I considered the implications of my personal history.

Kade Nevala said lamias were feared and hated. Killed on sight, it sounded like.

Without someone like Dad to teach me how to care, how to draw upon my humanity as a balance to my snake side, how might I have turned out?

Cold.

The inner voice spoke with absolutely certainty.

There's a reason "cold-blooded" is used to describe sociopaths.

I shivered a little as I pulled my pants up over my hips, despite the remaining warmth from the heat lamp and my quickly-warming mammal blood. Without my parents to guide me, I would never have learned to have compassion for the people with whom I interacted every day.

And the children I worked with now? How would I feel about them?

Prey.

I sent up a tiny, thankful prayer to whatever deity might listen to a weresnake raised as a human.

As I opened the shed door and stepped out into the last rays of the sunlight, I realized something important.

I had never actually asked Kade if the murdered girls were shapeshifters.

I had assumed it, but I hadn't gotten confirmation.

I needed to know for sure.

And I needed to know how likely it was that a shapeshifter was the one hunting them.

If I could imagine seeing them as prey, surely other shifters could, as well.

~

"HEY, LADYBUG!" Mom called out as soon as I opened the back door. She was bent over, digging around in the refrigerator for salad ingredients, judging by the plastic box of baby spinach she held out behind her. "See if that's still any good."

I took it from her and opened the lid, peering inside. "You hid it from yourself in the rotter again, didn't you?"

"It's called a crisper, smartass." She came up with a bag of carrots and a single zucchini squash, only slightly shriveled at one end. "Check these, too, while you're at it." Pushing her glasses up on her nose and patting her graying brown hair back into place, she peered around the kitchen. "What did I do with the pepper?"

If Dad was the heart of our little family, Mom was the brains—just not in the usual sense. Also a college professor, she was a true intellectual, at least inasmuch as she spent most of her time up in her own head. She always said Dad kept her grounded. Dad joked that her version of grounded was only halfway into the stratosphere. She was an astrophysicist. They had met in graduate school, and she had followed him to the plains of North Central Texas to support his career, rather than heading off to work for NASA or someplace with a good telescope. That's how I knew for sure that she loved him. And how I knew he loved her? He supported her every summer as she headed off to those fabulous telescopes to do her research, then welcomed her home again every fall when she returned to teaching classes at a local college and to him.

Still in love, after all these years.

Yet another way they taught me about being human.

And for the first time, it occurred to me that Dad's love of snakes, with their apparent disinterest in him, might have made him Mom's perfect partner.

Today was a day for all kinds of revelations.

I moved to the sink to check the vegetables, rinsing and scrubbing the useful ones, tossing the rest into the compost bin.

Mom finally located the pepper and began twisting the grinder over the steaks. "How's work?" she asked.

"Weird," I said, after a long moment. Flicking a spinach leaf going to slime into the silver, plastic-lined trash can on the counter, I added, "We're working with the police on some murder cases."

Despite her usual acceptance of the fact that most of my work was strictly confidential, this gave Mom pause. "Anything you can talk about?"

"Not about the case itself, exactly. But there's something I want to discuss with you and Dad."

"Okay." She took a plate out of the cabinet. "Over dinner." With a fork, she stacked the three steaks onto the dish, then handed it to me. "Dad's got the grill going. Take these to him."

I stared down at the meat. "How did you know I was coming?"

A beatific smile floated across her face. "Mother's intuition."

"Seriously, Mom?"

This time, she gave a shrug and a laugh. "Okay. There's a meteor shower tomorrow night. I'm hoping to take some students out to see it, and I thought it might be nice to make something for your father. Otherwise, he'll just eat a bowl of cereal while he reads the latest journals."

Yep. He might keep her grounded, but she took care of him, too, in her own way.

Everything I knew of love came from these two people.

And a giant albino Burmese python named Suzy.

∽

"So TELL us what's up at work," Dad said before scooping up the last forkful of steak from his plate.

I had no idea when Mom might have told him I was having work issues, but they often seemed to function in tandem like that.

When I was younger, I had sometimes wished for a partner like that—someone who could all but read my mind, who would know what I needed and offer it, just because he loved me.

That was before I learned the reality of my situation.

Before I figured out that I couldn't risk sharing my secret unless I also wanted to risk having that secret made public.

How could I be sure I could trust anyone with something that big?

But now, I knew there were other shapeshifters.

"It's not at work, exactly, though it's tangentially connected," I said.

"Sounds like it's something you want to avoid discussing." That was Dad all over—he inevitably went straight to the heart of the matter. Even though I had come out here planning to tell them everything, I didn't exactly want to talk about it.

Dad would say—had said, many times, when I was younger—that those were exactly the things that needed to be dragged out into the light.

As I had so often done before, I grit my teeth and blurted it out to them. "I met another shapeshifter."

Mom gasped, and Dad slowly lowered the napkin he had been using to wipe his mouth. Setting it carefully on the table, he tilted his head inquisitively. "Another weresnake?"

"No." I tried to decide how much to tell them. Kade hadn't exactly said that his own existence as a shifter was a secret, but everything about his actions thus far—along with the fact that there were no reputable news stories about shapeshifters among us—suggested that he wouldn't want me to tell anyone.

Finally, I settled on the generic outlines. "Another animal form, a mammal. He's a doctor, and we're working on a case together."

Mom shoved her glasses up. "How did you discover that he is also a shapeshifter?" Her voice was precise and direct. I could imagine her taking scientific notes as I spoke.

These were the only people in the world I trusted entirely. I told them everything I had learned so far from Kade. That I was a lamia, that lamias were considered extinct, that they were unwelcome in the shifter community at large.

As I wrapped up, Dad nodded thoughtfully. "I'm not entirely surprised. When no one came for you, I assumed that either your immediate family was gone, or that your kind didn't tend to its young for very long. Given your human form, the latter seemed unlikely."

"Did you suspect there were other shifters out there?" I tried to keep my tone level, but some of my outrage seeped through, anyway.

Dad raised one shoulder in a half-shrug. "It's a reasonable assumption, Lindi. It seemed at least possible."

"Well, I didn't." I slumped back in my seat. "I guess I didn't want to think about it at all."

"I was surprised that you never wanted to search out your birth parents," Mom said, standing to begin clearing plates from the table. "Most adopted children do, you know."

I rose to help, gathering the salad bowl from the middle of the table. "Most adopted children don't have to consider the difficulties of searching for a snake family."

61

"So you did consider it, then." Dad followed us into the kitchen, opening the refrigerator to put away the dressing and butter.

In another family, this might have been an uncomfortable discussion, but Mom and Dad had always supported me. My decision to avoid researching my roots had been perfectly logical.

Or at least, I had thought so at the time.

Now I wondered if I had been frightened of what I might find.

Dad's next statement drove that idea home. "You know I would have helped you. We might not have found anything, but we could have searched together."

I closed my eyes briefly as I nodded. "Yeah. I know."

"Do you want to try now?" His warm hand on my shoulder felt like support, but tears pricked my eyelids, anyway.

"I think maybe I'd better not."

If they were really all dead, it would be like losing them all over again—and for the first time.

And if they weren't dead?

I was afraid that finding them might be dangerous to us all.

CHAPTER

TEN

The next morning, Kade and I found something in the CAP-C files almost immediately.

I had been reading out client names from the file headers, becoming increasingly bored with the repetitious work, when I said, "Preston Bryant."

"Wait." Kade flipped through a computer printout he'd been perusing. "Bryant? Open that one. Check for a sister? A Kirstie."

I scanned the intake socio-economic information. "Yep. She's right here."

"Then we've got a match." He glanced at the rest of his list. "So do we keep going, or do we call in reinforcements?"

I hadn't asked before, had been almost actively restraining myself from it, but now I had to know. "Are the Bryants shapeshifters?" I whispered as I leaned toward him, glancing at the open door.

His gaze flicked to the door and back, too, and he nodded, holding up one finger.

Picking up a pen, he scratched a word onto a sticky pad next to him.

It took me a moment to work out what it said.

Definitely a doctor's handwriting. Or maybe a mongoose's.

Wait.

Fine. But I wasn't planning to wait for long.

LATER, after Kade had left for a shift at the hospital, I had three back-to-back CAP-C appointments. Two were court-ordered evaluations, the first for a divorcing couple in a custody fight, the second for a toddler, a little boy whose father had been accused of physical abuse. The final meeting of the day was with a teenage girl whose sexual-abuse outcry against a teacher had gained some media attention recently. It had also led to some pretty vicious threats from classmates who called her a liar, among other things.

All in all, it was about as rough as my days got—or at least, as rough as they had gotten before I had to spend my time looking at slides of dead girls.

By the time midday rolled around, I was ready to be left alone with the silence in my mind, so when Gloria stuck her head in and asked, "Want to get lunch today?" I simply groaned in response.

"That bad?" she asked.

"Worse. I'm going to stay behind and catch up on paperwork here."

My boss waggled her fingers in farewell and shut my office door behind her.

I hadn't been entirely honest, though.

Peeking out the curtain over my window, I waited for everyone to pile into their cars and drive away.

Then I began watching the YouTube videos I had

searched for that morning, before the parade of children in pain had begun its march through my office.

Every single video was entitled Mongoose vs. Snake— or some version of it.

And in all of them, the mongoose won.

I hadn't really known what a mongoose looked like. In my mind, they were long and wiry, like a weasel. I hadn't been entirely wrong, but the animals in these clips were more muscular and compact.

And fast. Damn, were they fast.

The snakes didn't have a chance.

I watched the golden-furred creature in the latest video leap out of the way of the striking cobra. It used the serpent's movement as a chance to bite down, just behind the head, rendering the snake helpless.

The skin on the nape of my own neck prickled in response.

Where were the videos where the snake won? Did people hate snakes so much that they refused to upload videos with different outcomes?

Or was this the inevitable end of any conflict between mongoose and snake?

The virtual extinction of lamias suggested that the mongoose always won.

After all, Kade hadn't mentioned his people being wiped out.

"Screw this," I muttered, closing out the window.

Most of the records of the murdered girls' families were gone. Jason and Scott had taken the primary files to the DA's office. But I still had my case notes, the ones I used to write up my reports. Flipping through the records for Preston Bryant's family, I found an address.

I was beginning to be certain that all of these people were shapeshifters.

So why had none of them recognized me as a lamia? Why only Emma Camelli and Kade Nevala?

I didn't see any other connections among the families. Jason and Scott hadn't, either.

But maybe, now that I knew about the shifters, I could find out something that the ADA and the investigator couldn't.

A glance at my calendar showed me that my next appointment wasn't until 2:00.

I scribbled out a note to let Gloria know where I'd gone and stuck it to her office door on my way out.

THE STREET LEADING to the Bryant's home started out narrow and paved, albeit cracked, but petered out to a rutted track in the weeds by the time it reached their yard. Like many in this neighborhood, the house itself had once been a mobile home, but was now permanently settled on this scrap of rocky land.

I hadn't been out here before, and even if I had, Gloria or one of the other counselors would have come with me. Home visits weren't unusual, but we rarely made them alone. Occasionally, parents were less than thrilled with the information their children gave out in counseling. Often, they were afraid that we would call Child Protective Services to take their children away.

Sometimes we did.

There hadn't been any notes in the file about the Bryants having any such concerns. And although it had been almost a year since I had seen them, I recalled then-ten-year-old Preston Bryant as being clean and well-spoken. My memory of his sister Kirstie was fuzzier. I had spoken to her only once or twice. The family had landed in my office when a neighbor's gun-shooting rampage had ended with the boy taken hostage for an hour before being shoved out the door as the neighbor shot himself.

The family had been too poor to pay for counseling services, but the mother had persevered until Victim's Services had referred them to us.

Not once had I suspected they might be anything other than they appeared: a poor, but loving family of humans.

And there had been no indication that they recognized me as a fellow shapeshifter.

Leaving my car in the overgrown grass of the yard, I picked my way to the rickety steps leading up to the tiny landing at the front door. The doorbell didn't echo inside the house, as far as I could tell, so I pulled open the screen and knocked on the door, as well.

While I waited, the screen door propped open against my back, I opened up my serpent senses to see if my animal side could detect anything unusual.

No additional body heat anywhere nearby, though the sun shining down warmed the top of my head.

I licked my lips, letting my tongue linger long enough to taste the air around me.

Grass. Dirt.

The mechanized smell of oil and gas coming from my car, still warm in the yard. The pickup beside it had been cold for some time.

People.

And under it all, something else.

Something wild.

Not spicy and hot, like Nevala, but not completely different from him, either.

Fur and claws.

Something feline.

The door swung open just as I recognized the scent, and

Preston Bryant froze in place, hand still on the door, eyes wide as he stared at me.

"Move, Preston. It's that counselor. Let me say 'hi'." His little sister shoved him two stumbling steps sideways to take his place. She drew in a deep breath to speak to me, but the words never came.

Whatever she identified in that breath, whatever her shapeshifter senses picked up from me, pushed any other considerations to the side, and instead of saying something, she screamed.

It wasn't an ordinary scream, either—nothing that could have come from the throat of a six-year-old child. It echoed through the neighborhood with a snarl at the end of it.

I recognized that sound. Not from my shapeshifter senses, but from having spent summers camping with my father as he searched for new specimens, as far outside of civilization as we could get.

It was the scream of a bobcat.

CHAPTER
ELEVEN

I stared at the little girl in horror, even as my own inner snake reared up, trying to take over. My vision shifted between colors and gray as I fought against the shift.

"It's me. Lindi Parker. I'm here to talk to your parents." The strain of fighting the shift echoed through my voice. A door in the back of the house opened, and the temperature of the room rose at the same time the scent of feline against my tongue intensified. I tamped down harder on my serpent side, even as the children's mother, in what I now recognized as her human form, padded into the room, accompanied by a full-grown bobcat by her side.

"Step away from the door, kids." She reached out and gathered her children to her, then gently pushed them into the room behind her. The girl's hand trailed across the bobcat's back as she passed him.

I held myself perfectly still as Rita Bryant's gaze ran up and down me, landing finally on my face, her brows knitted in confusion. "This isn't new, is it," she said, the words more statement than question. Running her hands through the fur of the cat beside her, she asked, "How did we miss it before?"

She didn't seem to expect an actual answer, so I simply turned my palms up in a gesture somewhere between *I don't know* and *I come in peace*. "I'd like to discuss that, if you're willing."

At her glance over my shoulder, I stiffened, uncertain whether it would be wiser to turn or stay perfectly still. As a compromise, I allowed just a tiny sliver of my inner snake to seep to the surface to test the air.

A blast of heat and fur slammed into me, overriding all other sensory input, and I carefully twisted around to look behind me.

While I had been stifling my inner nature in an attempt to radiate non-threat to the Bryants, at least a dozen bobcats had flowed silently into the grass between me and my car. Three or four of them were sitting, tufted ears perked forward. But the rest crouched, back ends twitching as they prepared to pounce.

As a child, I had gone through a phase of desperately wanting a kitten, but Dad had reminded me that I was likely to frighten any cat.

These cats weren't frightened. But I was terrified.

I wasn't used to being prey.

Human. I am human.

Turning my back on those glowing, predatory eyes was the hardest thing I've ever done.

I drew on every ounce of counselor training I'd ever had and focused on infusing my voice with it. "Ms. Bryant, I would never hurt you or your family." I spoke softly. "I am here to help you. I promise. Please talk to me."

The bobcat beside her growled a little, an answering wave of heat behind me alerting me to the other cats as they took a step forward.

Rita Bryant held up one hand. "You were a shifter when you helped us before. Why didn't you tell us?"

"I didn't know."

Another low growl, another wave of heat.

"I mean I didn't know that your children were shifters. I knew I was, of course. I thought maybe I was the only one." *Calm, Lindi. Remain calm.*

The sound of a car bumping up the lane made me want to turn around and look, but every instinct I had insisted that I remain perfectly still. No one else moved, either, not even when the vehicle pulled into the Bryants' yard and stopped.

Finally risking a glance behind me, I realized that the black Jeep had parked behind my car.

Great. Now I'm blocked in.

I had turned back to face the Bryants, when the slamming of the Jeep door brought a different scent to me— spicy, hot, and unmistakable.

Kade Nevala.

I couldn't decide whether to be irritated or thankful.

Maybe a little of both.

"Hello, Rita," he called out.

"Dr. Nevala." Ms. Bryant said, her tone neutral.

"Hi, Lindi," he said, all too cheerfully for my taste.

"Kade." I aimed for a flat tone, but a slight quaver ran through the word.

He moved up onto the tiny porch beside me, opening the screen door wider and placing a hand on my back in an oddly comforting gesture of support. "What do you say we take this inside?"

When he took one step into the house, the Bryant family backed up, just a little. Kade's fingertips exerted the tiniest bit of pressure, and I followed him. Inside seemed safer than outside, anyway. At least in here, there was only the one fully shifted bobcat. One set of claws to dodge, rather than a dozen.

Before he shut the screen behind us, Kade spoke to the assembled cats. "You're all welcome to stay, of course. We may be a while, though. And I give you my word that your clansmen and kits will be safe." He smiled, his voice dropping once again from formal into cheerful. "And you might want to see what you can do to be a little less conspicuous. I could see you from half a block away. Your neighborhood is private, but it's not that secluded."

At his words, the bobcats began to melt away, until only two remained, and those two laid down in the tall, slightly browned grass so that only someone actively looking for them would notice the black-and-tan fur pattern and ear tufts among the native vegetation that passed for a yard.

With a sigh of relief, I let Kade shut the door behind us.

I was totally unprepared when he spun on me and grabbed my upper arms, almost shaking me in his anger. "What the hell were you thinking?" he demanded. "You could have gotten yourself killed. Or worse, exposed these people to the rest of the world."

I shrugged him off, his accusations kindling an answering anger in me. "I knew these people, Kade. I worked with them for months, had no indication at all that they might be dangerous. And you, with all your secrets. I don't see you offering up any information about who's a shifter and who's not. It's not like I had any information to go on at all. So this is all your fault."

Rita Bryant interrupted my mini-tirade. "Dr. Nevala? I think we could use an explanation here. I'm right, aren't I? This woman is a lamia." She paused, eyeing me up and down again. "What is she doing here? Why is she still alive?"

The little girl, who had been standing silently, peeked

around from behind her mother. When she spoke, she flashed tiny elongated fangs—the kind of partial-shift hangover I remembered from my own childhood. "Yeah, Dr. Nevala," she said. "Why haven't you killed the bad snake lady yet?"

At her words, Kade grabbed me again, though this time the impetus behind it seemed more like protection than irritation.

I pushed out of his hold, anyway. "What are you doing here? How did you even find me?"

He unclamped his clenched jaw only long enough to respond. "I'm on the evening shift tonight at the hospital. I thought I'd drop by your office to see how you were doing. Everyone was returning from lunch, so I followed them in. Instead of you, I found a note announcing that you were coming out to visit some of the very people you were supposed to be avoiding."

"Avoiding? You're working with her?" Rita Bryant stepped in close enough to keep from being cut out of the conversation. Part of me was glad she no longer felt threatened by my presence. The rest of me wished she'd shut up so I could have it out with Dr. Mongoose.

"Let's all have a seat and talk about this like rational humans." Kade's voice was back to being warm and coaxing. My head spun with his changing verbal cues.

"Do you know what she is?" Rita Bryant demanded again.

"Yes. And I know something about *who* she is, too," the doctor replied. He took another step inside, and I followed him. The Bryant family fell back at our inexorable approach, but not in fear. I tasted the air, found something buttery and smooth flowing between Kade and the Bryants.

It was respect, I realized. They respected the doctor, this strange mongoose shifter who had followed me out to their home. I might have frightened them, but if he said I was trustworthy, they were going to believe it.

At least somewhat. The bobcat still carefully kept himself between me and the children, and when Rita tried to step forward, he sat down on her feet. We all stared at one another for a long moment. "Johnny," Rita finally said, "why don't you go on back and change. Dr. Nevala is here, and he'll watch us. We're okay."

After a long, hard look at me, the cat padded away. "Y'all have a seat," Rita said, gesturing toward the living room area. "I'll get us something to drink. And Johnny's going to need food. You want anything?" Her words were directed at the doctor. She wasn't comfortable enough to speak directly to me, at least not in any hospitable way.

But Kade glanced at me, taking in the short shake of my head before answering for both of us. "No, thanks."

The children sat huddled on the couch, staring at me as if we hadn't spent hours together in my office working through the trauma of Preston's kidnapping.

A sudden thought made me sit up straight, and the children both jerked a little. "Last year," I said. "The man who held you hostage?" It had taken us two weeks to come up with a term Preston could live with—something that allowed him to deal with his trauma, but did not, as he said, make him "feel like a baby." Thus "kidnapped" had been eliminated. "Besides," he had said, "he didn't take me anywhere. We were right in my living room."

This living room, I realized, looking around with new eyes.

"What about that man?" Rita said, her tone riding the line between polite and hostile.

"Was he a shapeshifter, too?" I held my breath, waiting for the answer. Would the knowledge have changed anything about how I had counseled Preston? Probably not.

"No." Rita's reply was short.

"But he saw Preston shift," Kirstie offered. Rita shook her head at her daughter, but in the irrepressible way of children, Kristie burbled on. "Mr. Vazquez moved in next door without getting the clowder's permission first, 'cause he didn't know he needed it, and by the time they found out, it was too late, but then he was out in his back yard, and he seen Preston turn cat."

With a sigh, Rita moved toward the kitchen.

Kirstie leaned forward, confidingly. "Mr. Vazquez was peeing. Outside. In his own human shape."

"He didn't have any other shape, dummy," Preston said, bumping his sister with his shoulder.

I had heard the part about the kidnapper's tendency to urinate outside. No one had mentioned any other shapes in our counseling sessions.

This kind of information-spilling was probably why I had seen Kirstie only occasionally during my time with Preston.

Rita came back in with a pitcher and passed around lemonade, giving up on trying to keep her daughter quiet.

Attempting to keep the children quiet was useless, of course. I had heard the rest of the story, anyway. And the longer I sat there with them, the more the Bryant children fell into their old habits of confiding in me.

I felt myself relax.

This will be okay.

And then Johnny Bryant walked into the room in, as Kirstie would have said, his own human shape, wearing nothing but a low-slung pair of jeans.

I was beginning to realize that although our shifter and human shapes were different, there were some similarities. Like a bobcat, Johnny Bryant wasn't particularly large, but he was muscular and compact. Like Kade, he radiated more power than his size should have allowed—unlike Kade, though, that power didn't call to me in any way.

"What is she doing here?" Johnny Bryant asked, running a hand through his tawny-blond hair.

"I came out to talk to the children," I began, but the bobcat shifter cut me off.

"I wasn't talking to you," he said.

Kade's calm reply helped me maintain my own cool. "She really is here to talk to the kids, Johnny."

"You vouching for her?" The man's scowl suggested that having Kade speak up for me would only barely make up for my mere existence.

"Yes." The single syllable sent a wave of relief through me. I hadn't realized until now exactly how anxious I had been that Kade might not fully believe me when I said I had no desire to hurt anyone.

"We should report her to the Council." Rita's soft tones cut through Johnny's masculine glare.

"Absolutely not," Kade said. "She hasn't done anything to hurt anyone. I will *introduce* her to the Council soon. Anyway, if I understand correctly, she did quite a lot to help your children last year."

Preston, still sitting on the couch, had unthinkingly reached down to clasp his sister's hand. "She did, you know," he said. "We talked about how I was held hostage, not kidnapped, and that the bad man was gone, and none of it was my fault. And she has a lot of toys in her office." His spirited defense of me made me smile, and he essayed a shaky grin back at me.

His mother, watching the exchange, said hesitantly, "She did help Preston." Her eyes narrowed and she spoke more forcefully. "But I still don't know how we missed what she is. And I don't know how you can stand to be around her." She pointed at Kade. "Aren't you supposed to protect us from things like her?"

I froze at the way she spat out the word 'thing.' As if I weren't a real person at all, despite all the ways I had helped her family.

Despite the fact that we were both shapeshifters—that both of us might be considered 'things' by the humans surrounding us.

But Kade's measured response ignored all those things. "I'm supposed to protect the entire community from dangers. I don't think Lindi is a danger to any of us."

I did my best to look unthreatening, clasping my hands in my lap and clamping down internally on every serpentine instinct I had, despite the almost overwhelming urge to open up and take the temperature of the room.

Hot, I was guessing.

I could almost imagine the scents of anger and fear.

But imagining was all I would allow myself to do.

I didn't know what this Council Rita had mentioned might do if they discovered a lamia in their midst, but I was fairly certain it wouldn't be anything good.

There had to be a way to keep the Bryants from sharing what they knew about me.

Because if they did, I was likely to be in big trouble.

I didn't relax until Johnny Bryant slumped back into a blue recliner, his posture apparently calm—but I could read the tension underneath the lazy pose.

Like a cat watching potential prey.

"Fine," he said, a wave of his hand encompassing both Kade and me. "Talk."

"Maybe we should let the kids go play or something," I ventured, uncomfortable making suggestions, but equally unwilling to let the children hear about the child-murders

—particularly Preston, who almost certainly still carried trauma from his kidnapping.

Rita nodded and jerked her chin at the two younger Bryants, who reluctantly stood. When they moved toward the back of the house, Rita stopped them. "Oh, no. You can still hear every word from back there. Go outside. I'll tell you if you need to know any of this."

They might have been powerful shifters, but the children still slumped off with typical protests.

All the adults remained silent until the front door shut behind Kirstie and Preston.

I let Kade do most of the talking, too worried about saying something that would set the Bryants off to do much but nod as the mongoose shifter gave a quick explanation of the potential connection between a series of shifter-victims, the hospital, and the CAP-C.

The mention of my employer caused the two adult Bryants to turn steely eyes on me.

"You ever think maybe she's doing it?" Johnny asked Kade, nodding toward me.

Kade replied without looking in my direction. "I'm certain she's not. Lindi has alibis for at least two of the times of death. She was with clients. I'm confident the detective in charge of the case will clear her of all the others, as well."

I had been examining the room, quietly trying to superimpose the image I had developed of Vazquez's kidnapping of Preston onto this real space, when Kade's comment pulled my attention back around to him. I hadn't realized that I had ever been under consideration.

It made sense, of course, that Kade would look into my background and any alibis once he made the connection between the CAP-C and the shifter-children's deaths.

Didn't mean I had to like it.

"So why are y'all here?" Rita asked as her husband settled back into the chair.

That *y'all* made me feel better than anything that had happened since I arrived on the Bryants' doorstep, indicating as it did Rita's lumping together of me and Kade.

Kade continued his explanation. "Lindi and I have been going through our files together to search for potential victims with connections to both the hospital and the CAP-C. This morning, we found Preston's files. We're concerned that Kirstie might be in danger."

This time, the low, inhuman growl that filled the room came from Rita, not Johnny. Her green eyes glowed, the light reflecting off the cat's pupil in her otherwise human face.

"The clowder protects its kits," Johnny said, his tones guttural.

"As do all the other shifter clans." Kade leaned forward to emphasize the words, despite his mild tone. "We simply want to add to that protection."

"How?" The single word hissed out around sharpened teeth that flashed when Rita spoke.

"Our best bet is to catch whoever is doing this." I spoke for the first time since Kade had taken over. "Can you think of anything that might help us with that?"

Johnny snarled, and the temperature of the room rose. Kade placed one hand on my arm. "We understand you might not be able to come up with anything right now," the mongoose shifter said. "We'll leave your den now. If you think of anything that might help us, you can call me. Will that work?"

Johnny nodded and Kade rose, pulling me with him.

"Thanks," Kade said as we moved toward the door. "We appreciate anything you can tell us."

We shut the door behind us, and I glanced around the

yard. I could hear the Bryant children's voices rising in play from behind the trailer. The two guardian cats were still in place, perfectly motionless except for their heads turning to track me as I moved toward my car.

"I'm sorry," I began, but Kade cut me off.

"We can discuss it back in your office," he said curtly.

I wasn't looking forward to that conversation, but I didn't say anything else in front of the unknown shifters watching us.

TWELVE

When we returned to the CAP-C, we didn't get to have the conversation I really wanted—the one where I confirmed that someone really was killing shifter children who had been both Kade's patients and my clients.

Instead, Scott was waiting when we arrived, seated in a chair in my office, his legs stretched out before him, his booted feet crossed at the ankles, hands clasped behind his head, elbows out. When he saw Kade walk in behind me, Scott's eyes narrowed, but he didn't move otherwise.

"You two find anything interesting?" he asked.

Kade shook his head. "The Bryants couldn't think of anything that might help us."

Now Scott did move, standing in one fluid motion. "You should probably leave the questioning of potential victims to the experts," he said.

The comment made me snarl, even though I suspected it was directed more at Kade than me. Still, I couldn't let it go. "I am an expert," I reminded him. "I've questioned dozens of victims and potential victims right beside you. Even more without you around."

Scott's slightly belligerent posture relaxed as he turned his attention to me. "You're right, of course. Sorry about that, Lindi."

"No problem." I moved around behind my desk, trying not to let the exchange bother me. I could at least ignore it. "You have something new for us, or are you just here to visit?"

Kade eyed the taller man for a moment, then took one careful step back to stand behind Scott, almost fading into the corner of the room.

His bright eyes flickering around the room suggested he was taking in every nuance of the exchange, though.

"I stopped by to see if you'd turned anything up," Scott said.

"Not really." I fell into my usual report cadence, professional and clinical. "No one at the Bryants' could think of anything odd that has happened—and since their child's kidnapping, they've been pretty hyper-aware. They're watching even more carefully now, though."

"Good. Write up a report and send it to me. I'll let you know if we come up with anything."

"Thanks." I worked to keep my tone neutral.

With a nod, Scott rapped two knuckles on my desk. "Okay. We still on for tonight?"

At the investigator's words, a wave of spicy-scented heat rolled over me from Kade's corner. Even Scott felt it—his eyes flickered toward the corner and a tiny frown creased his brow, but he didn't say anything.

"Yes," I responded, a little too loudly and emphatically. Scott blinked and his eyes darted toward the corner again, but he simply nodded and moved toward the door. He stopped in the doorway, turning so his face was clearly visible to both me and Kade. "Looking forward to it," he said, and winked at me.

The tiny smile quirking his lips as he left the room was followed by another hot wave of anger.

∾

I NEVER DID GET to talk to Kade that afternoon. As Scott was leaving my office, Gloria came in to discuss a child-abuse case, and with a nod to both of us, Kade slipped out.

By the time I got home to my two-bedroom condo, all I wanted to do was collapse on the couch and recover from my day. Dealing with the Bryants' anger had taken a toll on me, and I could have happily spent the evening watching stupid television shows. Maybe a sitcom marathon, shows with no elements of crime or the supernatural.

I had promised to go out with Scott, though, so after only one half-hour episode, I heaved myself up and went in to take a shower.

The hot water pulled the worst of the strain out of my muscles, and by the time Scott arrived, I was ready, wearing my favorite little black dress and heels.

"You look great." Scott handed me flowers as I opened the door. It was a sweet, old-fashioned gesture, and I felt like I should probably appreciate it more. All it did was make me anxious about the possibility of ruining what had been, until now, a great working relationship.

After I put the flowers into a makeshift vase—a large mason jar that had once held salsa from my favorite restaurant—we climbed into his truck.

"A movie okay?" Scott asked.

"Sure. What do you want to see?"

He tossed out the name of the latest science fiction blockbuster.

Not likely to include much in the way of either crime or the supernatural. Almost as good as a rom-com.

I was right, too. The movie was nicely distracting and had the added benefit of keeping me from trying to talk shop with Scott, at least until dinner at a new Italian restaurant afterwards. Even then, I managed not to bring up work.

Scott did. "Learn anything interesting from the Bryants today?"

I twirled angel hair pasta around my fork, watching the tendrils wrap around one another as I tried to marshal my thoughts and the lies I would need to tell. "Not really. They're suspicious of anyone who comes to talk to them. Not Kade, though. He's treated the whole family before, I think."

Scott frowned at the mention of the doctor. "You've treated the whole family, too."

"But only after that one traumatic experience. It's not surprising that they might want to distance themselves from everything and everyone associated with that incident." I cut a tiny piece of chicken off the cutlet on my plate and added it to the twirled pasta. Popping it in my mouth, I waited to see if Scott had anything to add to his comment.

My mouth was so full that I almost choked when I looked up to see Kade standing behind Scott, glaring at me with eyes that shimmered gold and hot.

I managed to swallow down the food with a gulp of water just as Scott turned to see the doctor behind him.

"What's going on?" I asked at the same moment that Scott demanded, "What are you doing here?"

Kade's nod encompassed Scott, but he made eye contact with me when he said, "It's Kirstie Bryant. She's been attacked. We need to go to the hospital."

THE CHILD'S dark lashes threw spiky shadows across her cheeks. When Rita Bryant saw me enter the curtained enclosure in the ER, she stood up and growled, her entire body tensing as she bared slightly elongated and pointed teeth at me.

Scott's gaze flickered back and forth between us, confused but assessing.

Kade moved to intercept Rita before she got to me, placing gentle fingertips on her upper arms. "Remember, I said I'd deal with this."

The cat shifter's stance didn't change, but she nodded and took a step back.

"What's going on?" Scott addressed Kade, but his glance included me in the question.

"What happened?" I ignored Scott's question, focusing on Kade.

"This evening, sometime after we left the Bryants' home—"

"What time exactly?" Scott interrupted, then shook his head and raised one hand at his own question. "Scratch that. Give us the details first."

"At some point late this afternoon or early this evening, Kirstie was attacked."

"Fine. I'll get the timing details from the cops. What's wrong with her now, physically?" Drawing a small notepad from his back pocket, Scott began jotting down information.

"She's been poisoned." I heard the anguish in Rita's voice, coming out in a slight burring of her voice—the sound of an animal's growl underlying her human speech.

"With?" Scott didn't look up as he continued writing.

"Snake venom." Kade's eyes flicked toward me, then away again.

Scott's hand paused above the paper. "What kind?"

"We're not entirely certain, though we've given her a standard antivenin cocktail." Now Kade was the one reverting to a professional tone, as if to cover the potential oddities of the conversation.

Narrowing his eyes, Scott dropped his hands to his sides without putting the pen or notepad away. "If you don't know what kind of snake, how do you know it's snake venom?"

"There are bite marks on Kirstie's side." Kade pointed toward the bed, waving his hand from side to side to take in the tiny figure huddled under the covers.

"Show me," I said.

Kade glanced at Rita as if for permission. She pursed her lips, but nodded, and the doctor lifted the little girl's gown up on one side, high enough so I could see the double pair of fang-marks on her side. Whatever it was had struck just above the waistband, an area unprotected by her pants and easily exposed if she lifted her shirt.

I needed to talk to Rita Bryant, to learn more about what, if anything, she had seen, if Kirstie had said anything about her attacker.

I couldn't ask any of that in front of Scott—not if I wanted to get real answers.

But there was no doubt in my mind it was a lamia.

I had grown up with a herpetologist.

I not only was a snake in my other form, I also knew snakes, inside and out. I knew their fang tip spread, their venom strength, their muscle tone.

This was not a bite from a regular viper. The puncture marks were too far apart. The serpent that had bitten her was at least as big as Suzy, but with a venomous bite—and most snakes Suzy's size or bigger were constrictors, not vipers.

Except me.

This wasn't my bite, of course, and I suspected I could prove it—these fangs were farther apart than my own.

Scott stepped in. "Wait. I'm confused. She was snake-bit? What makes you think this is connected to the other attacks?"

Kade pulled back the curtain, and with a jerk of his chin, he indicated the nurses' station a few feet away. We followed him as Rita sank back into her chair, all of her attention focused once again on her unconscious child.

Kade leaned against the far edge of the counter, as far away from the busy, bustling doctors and nurses as possible. "The mother says she saw ... someone ... leaving the scene."

"So why did she come at Lindi when we arrived?" Scott asked.

"She thinks that the someone she saw might have been Lindi."

Something flickered through Scott's eyes as he glanced at me.

"A woman?" I asked. For some reason this surprised me —probably because statistically, most killers were men.

Then again, Kirstie wasn't dead.

"What time was this?" Scott was back to jotting in his notebook.

"Around seven o'clock."

"Then it couldn't have been Lindi. She was with me."

The air around us heated with Kade's anger, but his face remained perfectly expressionless. "She was?"

"We were watching a movie in a theater." I might have imagined the slight smirk that crossed Scott's face as he spoke, but I doubted it. "And then we went to dinner.

Where you found us." He paused for a moment, then spoke again. "How did you know where we were, by the way?"

"Lucky guess," Kade said shortly. "I called Detective Moreland, too. He should be here soon."

Scott raised one eyebrow at this non-explanation, but Kade and I both ignored him. After a moment, the investigator continued speaking.

"If the mom thought it was Lindi, that gives me at least one small detail to go on." Scott made a few more notes. "But damn," he said quietly. "I wouldn't have expected it to be a woman. These serial things are usually men."

Exactly what I had thought. But something else had occurred to me in the meantime, and I couldn't figure out any way to tell Scott that it really might be a man. If I read Kade's comments and expression correctly, what Rita Bryant had seen wasn't a person at all, but a snake.

A shifter snake.

And that could mean only one thing.

Somewhere out there were other lamias.

I wasn't alone.

But my relative, whoever and wherever he might be, really was a monster—the kind who killed little kids for fun.

"Guess I'd better go interview Mrs. Bryant." Scott's determined move toward the woman left me standing alone with Kade, my head spinning from the implications of what I'd learned.

"So," the doctor said. "Dinner and a movie with Scott?"

I blinked at him for a long moment before I finally replied. "Don't. You know what this might mean. Don't try to distract me, Kade."

"You tell me what you think it means." Kade crossed his arms and leaned back, those golden highlights in his eyes starting to churn as he stared at me. Momentarily distracted, I wondered what other people—non shifter people—thought of his strange, swirling eyes.

I lowered my voice. "It means there might be another lamia."

He nodded. "Why else do you think I asked you to come here tonight?"

"You mean, after hauling me into a room to maul me the other night? Gee. What else could I possibly think you wanted to discuss?"

Kade ignored my snarky comment. "I think maybe we should let the others know about you."

"What happened to *if they find out, you'll have to do your duty and kill me*?"

"The situation has changed." When Kade glanced up and waved at someone over my shoulder, I realized that we were standing only inches apart, hissing at one another.

No, nothing suspicious about that. Nothing at all.

"We need to have a long conversation, somewhere far away from anyone else involved in this case," I said, stepping away from him.

Kade ran his fingers through his hair, sighing. "Yeah. Soon."

"How much does Kirstie need you here tonight?"

His eyes widened in surprise. "Really, not at all. I've given her the best antivenin we have here for a lamia bite, and the nurses can watch her overnight."

"What do you mean, best antivenin you have here? Do you not have the best that exists?" It seemed to me that a hospital catering to shifters should have top-of-the-line remedies for shifter illnesses and poisons.

He shrugged. "It's been a while since we've needed it. What we had on hand was old, probably degraded. I gave her the last of it." He paused, glancing at me briefly, then continued. "We thought lamias were extinct. There was no need for any more. And no way to get more, as far as we knew."

I was beginning to come up with an idea, but it was one that I really didn't like very much at all. Still, I had to know. "Do you know how the antivenin is made?"

"Sure. All of my kind do. We develop it from the actual venom. ..." His voice trailed off.

Crap. I'd been afraid of that. "Would Kirstie benefit from a fresher dose?"

"Maybe, maybe not." The scent of his anger had long since faded, and his eyes had lost that golden churn. Now he stared at me worriedly.

I had to know. "If there's another lamia out there attacking people, will you need more antivenin?"

"Yes." His expression suggested more hesitation than his clipped response indicated.

The idea of suggesting what I was about to suggest made my stomach twist. But Kirstie lay perfectly still and silent in that hospital bed, much more frail than the rambunctious little girl of just a few hours ago. That change might be my fault. Whatever had attacked her—and from all indications, it really was a lamia—had done so after my visit.

Every one of the victims in the murder case was connected to the CAP-C and Kindred Hospital.

To me, and to Kade Nevala.

If there was something I could do to fix it, I had to do it.

"Come on," I said. "Let's go get some venom."

THIRTEEN

The startled look on Scott's face when I told him I was leaving gave way to a flash of irritation when I added that Kade was taking me home. I didn't have time for male histrionics, though, so I pretended not to see it, and Scott was adult enough to tamp down any jealousy he might have felt.

Kade led me to the Jeep in his assigned parking spot and held the door open for me. "I am sorry I interrupted your date," he said as he slid behind the wheel.

"I might have been happier if I'd been able to finish my meal before the crisis hit, but it's not like the timing is somehow your fault." My stomach chose that moment to growl, and Kade's lips quirked up in a flashing grin.

"Aren't snakes supposed to eat once a month or something?" His sidelong glance suggested he was teasing.

"I thought you were the lamia-killing expert."

"Emphasis on killing. We didn't really focus on the daily habits of our prey." His tone was light, but the words made me shiver.

"Where to?" he asked as he pulled out of the hospital parking garage.

I thought for a moment. The idea of suggesting his place made my knees quiver. It was why I had wanted to have our big conversation out in the open, someplace public enough that his scent wouldn't overcome my will to keep him at a distance.

That same scent that filled the car now, intensifying the longer we were together, the taste of heat and spice filling my mouth and shooting straight down to my stomach. It was all I could do not to moan aloud.

Dammit. I was supposed to be thinking of a place for us to go where I could shift safely, where we could arrange for him to harvest enough venom to save at least one little girl, maybe more.

"My parents' ranch." The answer came to me instantly —it was, after all, the one place I always felt safe.

And it was the last place I was likely to give in to the lust Kade evoked in me.

"Your parents?" In his surprise, he jerked the wheel of the Jeep, causing it to swerve a little.

"Don't lose it, Dr. Cool," I said dryly. "My adoptive parents. I don't have any idea who my biological parents were."

"Right," he muttered. "Of course not."

I watched the streetlights flicker across his face as he followed my directions and merged onto the highway. "And after we do this thing, I think it's time for you to tell me everything you know," I said. "I need you to tell me where I came from."

He didn't say anything, but his jaw tightened, and he nodded. "Making antivenin isn't easy."

"I'm well aware of that. My father's a herpetologist—

and he arranged for antivenin against my venom a long time ago, in case I ever bit anyone."

"Does he still have it?"

"I'm sure he must." I pictured his workroom, the carefully labeled boxes on the top shelf that ran all along the wall, the small refrigerator in one corner, the sealed safe in another. "I have some ideas."

"Anything we could get to soon?"

"We can go right now."

"And we can arrange for more, as well."

I HAD CALLED AHEAD to let Dad know we were coming out to the herpetarium, but he and Mom had gone out for the evening. "You know how to get in," he said. Just before I disconnected, he asked, "Is this someone we need to meet?"

"I don't know yet," I said, and as usual, he accepted my word.

My parents' absence somewhat limited the psychological dampening effect on any desire I might have to shove Kade up against the wall and have my way with him—or let him have his way with me. I hadn't realized quite how much I had been counting on that parental inhibitor until I realized I was imagining licking the doctor's neck, pulling that taste into myself.

"Whatever you're doing over there, please stop," Kade said, his voice tight. With his left hand, he thumbed the control that lowered the window, letting in a rush of warm evening air. I found it surprisingly comforting that he was as obviously affected by me as I was by him.

"Sorry," I said, lowering the window on my side and letting the wind blow through my hair. The lingering scent of Kade swirled away on the breeze, and I found it easier to think.

Whether Kade was glad, I didn't know, but he didn't say anything else until we had pulled up in front of the house and he followed me around to the shed in the back.

When I opened the door and flipped on the light, he rocked back on his heels. "What the hell is this place?"

"Come on in and see," I said. The herpetarium, as familiar and calming as usual, put me at ease, and I turned to smile at Kade. That smile faded when I realized how tense he was. His light brown eyes were spinning with golden swirls, and his hands were clenched into fists beside him.

"It's okay," I said, trying to use the same tone Dad had always taken with me. "Remember, you're human. That's the part of you that's in control." Slowly, I reached out and took his hands into my own, drawing him into the room. "They're just animals. They're not a threat. You're in charge."

As Kade stared into my eyes, his breathing slowed to match my own. The churning in his eyes slowed, then stopped.

Finally, he relaxed.

"This is where you grew up?" he asked.

I could feel the thump of his heartbeat through his wrists where my fingers touched them, feel it slow as his breath evened out.

"Well, not in this room. I had a real kid's room in the house, full of Barbie dolls and Tonka trucks and Hot Wheels." I loosened my grip on him as he pulled away, my fingertips trailing across the tops of his hands. "My mother was determined not to give in to the 'gendering of America's children'. " I made air-quotes with my fingers.

Kade nodded absently as he moved from tank to tank,

peering in through the glass. "How many of these are poisonous?" he asked.

"To people? I never counted." I counted off on my fingers. "The copperheads, the rattlers, the water moccasins . . . "

"You have all of those here?" Kade leaned sideways to peer into the rattler tank.

"At various times. Dad's a scientist, but he loves the snakes, too, so he generally ends up letting them back out into the wild."

The doctor gave me a sidelong look. "But not you."

"Yes, he loves me, too." My tone was dry. "But no, he never had any intention of sending me back out into the wild by myself. Not once he realized what I was."

"Mm." Kade continued his circuit of the room. "He catches them himself?"

"Mostly. He's particularly interested in the effects of serpentine parthenogenesis, so recently he's been focusing on that. He's been setting the males free immediately."

Kade blinked, startled. "Parthenogenesis? I didn't know snakes could reproduce without male involvement."

"It's rare, but it happens." I drifted over to Suzy's tank and removed the lid, letting my hand slide over her. She bumped her head against my arm. "Hi, sweetie," I said softly. "Good to see you."

Kade finished examining the tanks and leaned back against the long, low table Dad used as a workspace. "You said there might be a stash of antivenin here?"

I moved to the tiny refrigerator where Dad kept all his supplies and pulled out a glass ampoule labeled with my name, and checked the date. "It's still good. We have enough for one patient." I considered for only a moment before speaking again. "We should get venom to make more to restock Kindred."

Kade nodded. "Thanks. How do we do that?"

"Here," I said, reaching past him into an overhead cabinet and drawing out two stoppered vials. "You'll use these." Bumping him out of the way with my hip, I opened a drawer and took out latex gloves, cling wrap, and rubber bands.

"Use them how?" He pulled on the gloves, then took the vials from me.

"You said you knew how the antivenin was made."

"How it's made, not how the venom is gathered."

"You won't have to do much." Kade held out the vials one at a time while I pulled the plastic wrap tight across the top opening of each and secured it with the rubber band. "Okay. After I shift, you hold the vials out. I'll bite them through the wrap. The venom should just flow into the tubes."

"And if it doesn't?"

I used my hands to indicate either side of my jaw. "There are glands roughly here, behind my head. Press down and forward along them. That should help." I demonstrated with my thumbs.

"What if you go for me instead of the vials?"

"I thought you were some big snake-killing shapeshifter. If I go after you, then you have my permission to stop me."

He smiled. "I'm probably immune—in the wild, a mongoose is usually resistant to the venom of the snakes it is most likely to come into contact with. Lamia venom rarely affects mongoose-shifters."

"Are you sure I can't hurt you?" I scowled.

"Not entirely. There are some subspecies differences."

"Then don't let me bite you."

"You mean I should kill you."

"Well, preferably not. But if I lose control and it's you or me? Then yes. You should do whatever it takes to keep me from hurting someone."

"You're not at all what I expected."

"Yeah, well, sometimes I'm not what I expected, either." My voice was soft. "Okay. Turn around, and don't look."

"Why not? It's not like I haven't seen you shift before."

"Yeah, but this time I'm going to strip first. It's easier if I don't have to fight my way out of my clothes afterwards."

"Oh." The single syllable was harsh, and Kade cleared his throat.

"What? Don't you take off your clothes before you shift?"

"Yes. Of course." Flustered, he turned his back to me.

It was probably cruel, but I took a little extra time taking off my clothes and folding them carefully, knowing that Kade was listening to every move I made. The lines of his back were stiff—and if the scents flowing off of him were anything to go by, that wasn't the only part of him standing at attention.

There came a moment, though, when I couldn't put off the shift any longer, and in the last grayed-out glimpse I got before the moment of terror took over and the change consumed me, I saw Kade's body language change from the stiffness of desire to the tense, straight-backed stance of fear, only barely under control.

When I could see again, Kade stood tall above me. I lifted the upper half of my body into the air, but I kept my distance, worried that he would mistake my stance for threat. Flicking my tongue out, I pulled in air molecules, sliding them over the Jacobson's gland on the roof of my mouth.

It was a relief to be able to analyze them directly. I could read the air so much more clearly in this form, where taste and smell combined into one. I had been right—the tart taste of Kade's fear as he turned his back on a lamia in mid-shift still lingered around us, as did the sharp heat of his desire for my human shape. But there was something else, too, rolling off him in waves as he knelt down beside me. In my human form, I would have considered it a blue smell, my shifter senses combining to create an odd synesthesia.

I recognized this scent. I had tasted it the first time Dad had watched me shift, and every time since then.

I had tasted it in the air the first time Kade had seen me shift.

It was wonder.

FOURTEEN

"Okay," Kade said, holding out the vials. "I'm presuming one per fang, right?" I nodded, my upper body bouncing and weaving just a bit.

"Here goes, then. Remember, bite the plastic, not me." A bright lance of anxiety drove through the blue scent when I stretched my jaws wide, but it retreated again as my fangs delicately pierced the cling-wrap covering the vials. Without any thought from me, the venom spurted out, my body jerking a little as the liquid pumped through me, soothing an ache I hadn't even realized was there.

Not for the first time, I wondered what it would be like to bite a living creature.

The thought both horrified and enticed me.

Dad had worked hard to teach me empathy, and part of that training had included forbidding me to hunt live animals in my serpent form. I understood the restriction, even agreed with it—but sometimes my serpent and human instincts warred with one another.

Kade moved closer to me so he could balance one of the vials against his knee and lifted a hand toward me, speaking softly. "I'm going to help, Lindi. This will pull more of the venom out, okay?" His voice dropped even lower. "I know you can hear and understand me. Please stay calm." Then his fingertips were pressing against the side of my head, behind my jaw, stroking firmly. The touch of his hand made me shiver, both in fear and anticipation, and I could feel my venom glands respond, pumping more and more of the viscous fluid through my fangs and into the glass vials.

"Good," Kade said softly. "Good. Now I'm going to do the other side, okay?"

The almost sexual anticipation sent a quiver down my entire body as he shifted around to make sure the vials stayed steady, then stroked the other gland. Again, my body responded instantly, sending more venom into the glass.

If I could have moaned in release, I would have.

God. Was this how I reacted to the touch of someone I was attracted to? Pumping out poison? And yet I couldn't help myself.

No wonder the rest of the shapeshifter world wanted everyone like me dead.

No. I had never bitten anyone. Never hurt anyone. I would never hurt anyone.

I couldn't help the physiological response. But I could be sure that it never happened except to help others. And that's what this was—an attempt to save Kirstie and anyone else like her.

Maybe I was a monster, but I could be sure to help rather than hurt.

I shuddered as the last of the venom poured out of me in an almost sexual release.

And then I pulled back, lifting away from the vials and coiling in on myself. The floor was cold and hard, and I wished I'd had the foresight to shift into Suzy's tank.

"Wow." Kade was peering into the vials, examining the thick, yellow liquid. "Yep. That's the stuff."

He stood up and carefully unwound the rubber bands, then peeled off the plastic wrap. He stoppered the vials.

"Now," he said. "I'm going to step outside while you change. And then we need to talk."

Five minutes later, I pulled my clothes back on, as weary and languorous as if I really had just finished having some sort of sexual experience. Or had eaten too much.

I didn't know if full-blood snakes felt that way, but I had often thought that it would explain their long sluggish periods after meals. I hadn't explained the question, but I had asked Dad why snakes took so much longer to digest their food than I did. He gave some long, semi-scientific explanation about the energy I used to shift and to maintain my warm-blooded side's body temperature. In the end, I finally decided the snakes had it better—and for a time as a child, I had refused to eat anything when I was in my human form. Except McDonald's chicken nuggets. Mom could always get me to shift for those.

I dropped the top back on Suzy's terrarium. "You be good. I'll come by later this week for a real visit." As ever, she radiated calm.

Pulling open the door and stepping out into the moonlit night, I followed Kade's scent—now back to his normal, everyday smell, slightly spicy and all male—around to the back of the herpetarium, where he stood staring up at the stars.

"Hey," I said, stepping up beside him.

"You know what that is?" he asked, pointing up into the sky.

"Sure. It's the Big Dipper." I extended my arm beside his. "And that's the Little Dipper. And over there is Cassiopeia."

He laughed. "I think that's the first time any woman has said yes to that question."

"Oh. I'm sorry. Was I supposed to go all feminine and fluttery and say no so you could teach me all about the stars?" I clasped my hands together under my chin and batted my lashes. I didn't know how much he could see in the dark, but I suspected his shifter nature meant that his night vision was as good as mine.

"God, no," he said.

"What will you do with that?" I asked, nodding at the vial of venom he still held. "We could ask my father to make the antivenin for us." My voice trailed off. I wasn't entirely certain how Dad had arranged for the last batch—it had been almost three years ago, and I hadn't really been paying attention. In fact, I had been irritated that he thought he needed antivenin at all, since I was completely sure that I would never, ever bite anyone.

And I hadn't. So far. But after years of dealing with the victims of pedophiles and abusers, I was less certain that I would never shift and attack. I could imagine circumstances that might call for it. I suspected I wouldn't even hesitate to attack if it meant saving one of my clients. Especially the ones who were too small to defend themselves.

"What would we need to do to make the antivenin ourselves?" I asked.

Kade swirled the venom around in the container, watching the viscous yellow liquid stick to the sides, then slide down. "It's a pretty labor-intensive process. Nothing we can do here."

"Where, then?"

"I'll have to take the venom back to my family home. It's something of the family ... business." An odd smile quirked his lip up as he spoke.

"So probably nothing I need to be involved in."

"You've done your part. We'll do ours next."

"Do we need to hurry? Do you need to get that to them now?" I gestured at the vials. "What about Kirstie?"

"The polyvalent antivenin she had earlier is good against lamias, and she can't have more for a while. It'll take some time to produce the new antivenin, and the first step is to freeze it. I've got dry ice in a cooler in the pickup. I'll go put this out there. I can drop you off at your place on my way. Unless you want to stay here."

"Let's get something to eat first—I'm starving. Want to go inside and see what my parents have available?"

"Sure." He fell in step beside me. "I don't know about you, but shifting always leaves me hungry."

So it was common. I had been so focused on figuring out what was going on with the children, with our case, that I hadn't even been able to figure out what questions I wanted to ask another shifter.

While Kade dropped the venom into the cooler, I stood with the back door propped open against my hip. Then he jogged back and followed me into the kitchen.

Opening the refrigerator, I rummaged around for a minute. "Beef fajitas work for you?" I asked, head still inside. I realized as I spoke how like my mother I sounded —and probably looked.

In the nature vs. nurture fight, nurture was definitely winning, right at the moment. I was definitely Mom's child.

The cast-iron skillet was in its usual spot in a bottom cabinet, and I took comfort in the familiar tasks. I put Kade to work chopping an onion as I sliced the beef and added spices to it. When I tossed everything in to sizzle, Kade pulled a barstool around from the other side of the counter and sat to watch me.

"So you really have no idea who your birth parents are?" he asked.

"Not a clue."

"Or if you were part of a . . . what do you call a bunch of baby snakes? A litter?"

I paused, lifting the spatula out of the frying pan. "Huh. I don't know. A baby snake is a hatchling. And a group of snakes is usually a nest. So I guess a nest of hatchlings?" I went back to stirring.

"Okay. So you don't know if you were part of a nest of hatchlings, or if you were a single birth?"

"Not a clue. I don't have any memories of the time before Dad found me."

"It just seems odd that a second lamia would show up right now, just as you did."

"You know, I didn't just 'show up'." I waved the spatula in the air, indicating the house around us. "I've been right here for the last twenty-five years. I grew up in this house. I belong here every bit as much as you do."

Because that was the crux of it, I realized. I'd been fighting off a deep, unspoken, almost unnoticed anger since I met the doctor—almost as much as I had been fighting off my attraction to him. The attraction was hard to explain. We should have been mortal enemies, but nothing in me wanted to hurt him. Not really. The anger, though? That was easier.

He knew who he was, where he belonged. He had grown up in an entire community of shapeshifters—one so big that they apparently had their own hospital, their own doctors, their own nurses. Hell, there were even entire neighborhoods chock-full of bobcat shifters, all ready at a moment's notice to circle around their own. To shift into their animal forms and protect one another.

And me? I had Dad and Mom. I was deeply thankful for them, for the way they had taken me in and made me part of their family. But becoming human for them had also meant giving up much of my shapeshifter instincts. It had been a long, hard fight, but I had done it. I had come off the ranch and into human society, where I was not only accepted, I was useful. Important. I helped human children move past their hurts and their traumas, past their anxieties and damage. Helped them to build new lives, stronger and better adjusted, part of the community around them.

Just like I had.

Then I discovered that there were other shapeshifters out there.

Other people who, like me, had to hide what they were if they wanted to fit in with the rest of society.

And in the very next instant, I had learned that these people, these shapeshifters, were every bit as afraid of me as any human could ever be. Maybe more so, because they knew what I was really capable of.

My years of training, of self-denial, of work and pressure, of hiding what I was until I had the iron self-control necessary to maintain my human shape in any situation?

None of it meant a damn thing.

I realized I was crying, tears dropping down to sizzle in the frying pan next to the onions and the steak strips, when Kade slipped up behind me and took the spatula from my hand. Without ever letting go of my waist, he gave the fajitas a final stir, then moved the skillet to a back burner and turned off the stove. Then he pulled me up against him, pulling my head against his shoulder, and wrapped his arms around me.

"It'll be okay," he whispered into my hair.

I wasn't sure I believed him, but I let myself sink into his comforting embrace, anyway.

After a moment, I dried my tears, sniffing. Kade handed me a paper towel from the dispenser by the sink, and I finished cooking.

We didn't discuss my weepy spell during dinner. Instead, Kade entertained me with stories of his days as a medical intern. He had completed a regular, human medical degree, then finished his training at Kindred, learning the specifics of shapeshifter medicine.

"So did you always know you wanted to be a doctor?" I asked as we sat in the living room after eating.

"From the time I was three, according to my family. I can't remember a time when that wasn't what I wanted to do." Kade leaned back on my parents' couch. Seeing him there, so strangely at ease in a space that had rarely seen anyone but my family and their colleagues, sent a flutter through my stomach.

I hadn't even dated in high school, and in college had never brought any of my boyfriends home to meet Mom and Dad. I knew what Dad would say—it wasn't safe, for me or the men I dated. Anything that might give away my secret was dangerous. And any chance that I might shift and hurt someone was to be avoided.

Not that I ever had. Even in the midst of toddler tantrums or teenage fits, I had never struck out at my parents. Even when I shifted in the midst of anger, I remembered enough to keep the people I loved safe.

What would it have been like not to have to remember that I could kill the ones I loved?

"Tell me about your family," I said.

"My family?" Kade kicked his booted feet up onto the ottoman in front of him, crossing them at the ankle as he stretched an arm behind his head and stared at the ceiling. "Well, there are a lot of us. In the wild, a mongoose litter is usually anywhere from two to five siblings, and that's something that crosses over to the shifters, lots of multiples."

"So you're, what? A twin? Triplet?"

He laughed. "No, I was a rare singleton. Apparently my mother was deeply disappointed when I was born. I'm the eldest, and she had been expecting a whole pile of babies. She got them the next two times, though. She had triplets two years after I was born. And quintuplets the last time."

"You have *eight* siblings?"

Kade misread the wonder in my voice. "Yeah. It's a lot of kids to raise."

But I was thinking of the amazing possibilities of that many children in the same family. What would it have been like to play with all those other kids? Learn with them?

"Are you all close?" I asked.

"Yeah." His smile turned inward. "Even when they drive me nuts. The triplets are all girls, and for the first several years of their life, I was convinced my parents had arranged to have them just to torture me. Everywhere I turned, there were dolls and dresses and three little girls wanting me to play dress-up with them." He laughed. "I used to shift to try to hide from them under the furniture, but then they shifted and dragged me out."

"Where did you grow up? Here in Texas?"

"There aren't actually a lot of mongoose shifters here. We didn't move to Texas until I was a teenager. No, I spent most of my childhood in Antigua."

"The island?"

"I miss the Caribbean. The beaches and ocean, of course, but mostly I miss not having to hide from anyone but the tourists."

"What do you mean? Did people there know what you are?"

"Absolutely. My parents were invited when a lamia clan moved in and started attacking locals. They had figured out that there weren't any natural predators on the island, so they stepped in and took over. The Antiguans were terrified, many of them convinced that some voodoo queen had conjured monsters to destroy them."

"Can people not fight against . . ." I paused, almost unable to say the word. "Against us?"

If Kade noticed my hesitation, he didn't mention it. "Not easily, though of course it's possible."

"So how did your family find out about it?"

"There were some other shifters on the island, and they contacted the Council."

"The same Council that the Bryants wanted to report me to?"

"A branch of it, anyway. So the Council sent out three mongoose families. Or rather, one extended family. Two of my uncles and their families, along with us."

"And what happened?"

"Oh. It took a little while, but my parents and aunts and uncles took out the lamia tribe. Though they lost one of my uncles."

"I'm sorry."

"It's part of the business." Again that quirk of the lip. "Not a happy part, but there you have it."

"Why do you grin every time you say 'business'?" I asked.

"Oh. That." The quirk turned to a full-blown smile. "Business is the collective noun for a group of mongooses. It's something of a family joke."

"And the collective noun for bobcats is clowder, right? The Bryants used the term several times this afternoon." I shook my head, almost surprised to realize that my almost-disastrous lunch visit had been less than twelve hours earlier.

"Each group has its own term, but we often refer to one another as 'clans' to cut down on any confusion. Makes it easier when there are cross-marriages, too—someone could join the bobcat clan even if they're not bobcats, and therefore not part of the clowder."

"Cross-marriages?" I tilted my head as I stared at him. "How often do those actually happen?"

Kade lifted one hand, palm up, as he replied. "My grandmother was a rabbit shifter."

I sat up straight and turned to face him directly. "You're not serious, right?"

Kade shrugged. "Shifter children can take on the animal form of either parent. My father inherited the mongoose shape."

"And if he'd been a rabbit?"

"Then grandmother would have taught dad how to be a rabbit shifter."

"That's not how genetics works." I was certain of it, based on what I'd learned in Biology 101. Then again, my college bio professors would have said I was impossible, if I'd ever tried to convince them I was a snake shifter.

Kade's laugh echoed. "Sure it is. There are dominant genes and recessive ones."

"You're telling me that if you had a child with another mongoose who had a recessive rabbit gene, you could end up with a rabbit-shifting child?" My tone almost managed to reflect my disbelief.

"Exactly."

"How would two mongooses even raise a rabbit?" I couldn't believe I was having this conversation.

"How do two red-haired parents raise a brunette? How do two athletic parents raise a bookworm? With love and care." He paused. "And if it were me, I'd probably be learning a lot about rabbits. But..." His voice trailed off.

"But what?"

"Rarely—very rarely—a child takes on both forms, becomes a chimera."

"A chimera?"

"The animal form is a combination of both parents. It's hard on the child, because they have to work particularly hard to avoid being seen by pure humans." He shrugged again. "That's what I'm told, anyway. I've never met one."

"You're telling me that I could have a ... a raccoon sibling out there and not even know it? Not be able to tell?"

"Honestly, it's unlikely. There are probably a few lamia crosses out there, but not many. The lamias were pretty adamant about keeping the bloodlines pure. That means that they rarely reproduced with anyone but other lamias, and the occasional human. Maybe pureblood snakes, too, but I don't know that for sure."

I stared at him blankly for a long moment. "Great. I'm descended from the shifter version of the Third Reich."

"Pretty much."

This whole examination of my heritage business was really starting to bother me. "So what else don't I want to know about the lamias? What else can you tell me about them?"

He dropped his feet to the floor and leaned forward. "For starters? I can tell you that I've never met one like you before."

"Like me?"

"Kind. Smart. Interested in saving people rather than hurting them."

"But you didn't know any of that the first time you saw me in the hospital."

"No."

"So why did you kiss me?" It was a question I had wanted to ask for days, ever since I had found out that we were supposed to be mortal enemies.

"That is an excellent question." He leaned forward even further.

"What's the answer?"

Rather than speaking, he slid out of his chair, landing on his knees in front of me. Placing one hand on either side of me, he pushed forward. I felt myself drawn to him, the heat of his body calling to me.

I opened my serpent senses, and as ever, the heat and scent of him washed over me. He moved slowly, giving me the opportunity to get away from him, but I didn't try to escape.

Our lips met, gently at first, then more firmly.

Kade pushed himself up, sliding one knee onto the couch between my legs. Wrapping one arm around my back, he pulled me closer to him, then shifted us around so I was lying on the couch beneath him.

And then he deepened the kiss, his hand sliding down to my thigh and pulling my leg up to wrap around him.

I sank into his heat, allowing it to permeate me, pour into me. His tongue swept into my mouth, tangling with my own. The taste of him made me whimper, deep in my throat.

I was only barely aware of the sweep of headlights sliding over us from outside until Kade broke the kiss. "Damn," he said. "I think your parents are home."

Damn, indeed.

Twenty-eight years old and caught making out on the couch.

Well, almost caught.

By the time Mom and Dad came in, Kade and I were sitting decorously apart again. He was back on the chair, and I had slid to the far end of the couch. I'd even had time to pat my hair back into place.

I don't know if they were fooled, but at least I didn't have to try to explain anything to them.

Other than my friend. The mongoose shifter.

Not that I said as much, but Dad guessed. He blinked a couple of times when he realized who Kade was, but simply shook the doctor's hand and asked if we were sure we needed to leave.

"Yeah. We just needed to stop by the herpetarium and snag some stuff." *More or less*, I amended silently.

"Okay, then." Dad's tone was mild, but his sharp glance suggested that he would have questions for me later. "Feel free to stop by anytime, Dr. Nevala. Lindi's friends are always welcome."

"Thanks so much, Dr. Parker. And please, call me Kade."

I appreciated Kade's use of Dad's title—an unnecessary courtesy, but one that showed the mongoose shifter's sense of propriety.

Sense of propriety? Oh, hell. I had to get us out of here before I let this turn into a full-blown *Meet the Parents* moment.

I ushered Kade out as quickly as I could, and we drove away with Mom and Dad standing on the doorstep, beaming after us.

It was as painfully adolescent as I could have imagined.

As we climbed into his truck, Kade stared at me thoughtfully for a long moment. He didn't speak until we were pulling out of the driveway and turning onto the highway. "I think it might be time for you to meet the Council."

FIFTEEN

I tried to ask questions, but Kade kept insisting that the Council was the next step.

We stopped by the hospital first, both to check on Kirstie and to make sure the first dose of antivenin hadn't had any adverse effects. Her parents still watched me warily, but this time I kept my distance.

Kade called a nurse over to him and they conferred briefly. "Continue to watch for any signs of a reaction, and contact me if necessary," he said to the dark-haired woman in scrubs. With a nod, she rolled a computer on a stand over to her and began entering the appropriate notes.

"How do you get away with it?" I asked as we left the hospital.

"Get away with what?"

"Having a hospital especially for shifters?" I pitched my voice low, trying to keep from being overheard.

He laughed. "It's not only for shifters. There aren't enough of us to warrant a whole hospital—and even if there were, we rarely get sick enough to need hospitalization."

"That makes it even stranger. How do you get away with a hospital that caters to shifters but still has human patients? That nurse was making notes in Kirstie Bryant's file. What if another doctor looked them up? Do all the doctors and nurses know about the shifters? How does this all work?"

Pulling his key-fob out of his pocket, he unlocked the truck. "I know you have a lot of questions. And I am more than willing to answer them. Just not all at once. And not until after you meet with the Council."

WHEN KADE SAID "THE COUNCIL," I could hear the capitalization in his voice, a respect echoing through his tone that caused me to expect a giant room with vaulted ceilings decorated in gold-leaf and a dais up at the front. In my mind, the Council members were dressed in long black robes—maybe even with white wigs. Like judges from some other country.

I was right about the vaulted ceiling. But it was over someone's lovely living room in a nice, middle-class neighborhood. A short, pudgy woman with an upturned nose and gray streaks through her dark hair opened the door. She glanced at me curiously when Kade introduced me simply by name, her blue eyes glinting behind round-rimmed glasses, but she led us in without comment and invited us to take a seat on the couch. I found myself scooting closer to Kade as other people filed in.

With each new arrival, the level of the energy swirling through the room spiked higher and the muscles in my back grew tighter as I fought off the urge to shift.

"You'll be fine," Kade murmured, dropping his hand down to rest on my own. I hadn't realized that I had grabbed the edge of the sofa cushion. I spread my fingers wide and smoothed down the brocade fabric.

I leaned in close to place my mouth almost directly to his ear, pointing my mouth down and toward the back of the couch in an effort to maintain privacy, all while knowing that some shifters' enhanced hearing might render the attempt useless. "How many of these people will want me dead?" I whispered.

"Doesn't matter. Council meetings are always peaceful. Everyone here has proven their ability to maintain control." Kade shrugged. "They may want to kill you, but they won't actually do it."

How reassuring.

Our hostess appeared with glasses of water, and I took one with a murmur of thanks. Then I stared into it, trying to decide whether or not to take a drink.

"It's not poisoned. Janice wouldn't be that subtle." Kade took a gulp from his, as if to prove his point.

"It's not that. I don't want to have to go pee in the middle of anything important." I tilted the glass, watching the light from the recessed fixtures overhead filter through it.

A sputter from Kade turned into a laugh as he shook his head. "And that's your biggest worry?"

"Hell, no. Not even close. But it's the only one I can control right now." Glancing up from my perusal of the glass, I saw one of the other shapeshifters watching me through narrowed eyes. Despite being slouched down into a chair in what should have been a relaxed pose, he radiated tension, from the way his stubbled jaw clenched to the constant tapping of his fingers on the armrest.

"Who's that?" I tried to disguise my question again, but from the man's sneer, I suspected he heard me. He definitely saw the little jerk of my head toward him, and when

Kade glanced at him, he nodded, the kind of bare, almost imperceptible nods that gunfighters always give one another in Westerns just before someone gets gunned down in the middle of the street. Come to think of it, he looked a bit like a young Clint Eastwood.

At Kade's whispered response brushing against my ear, a shiver ran down my arm. "That's Eduardo Valencia. He's one of the Council's Shields. Think protector. Guardian. He's the muscle."

A Council of shapeshifters who needed protection.

I wasn't prepared for that level of implied violence.

I might be a snake, but I wasn't a killer.

But the thought of it sent chills racing across my skin. If I were honest with myself, they were as much from excitement as fear.

Still, no one here needed to know that a part of me was drawn to the idea of violence.

It took about another ten minutes for everyone to arrive. The Council Shield watched me the whole time through his squinty, Eastwood-lookalike eyes. If not for Kade at my side, projecting authority somehow *out* so that his presence took up more space than his actual body, I might have bolted.

When had Kade become the force of reassurance in my life?

Sometime between *you're a lamia* and *everyone here wants to kill you*, apparently.

In any case, I was thankful for him.

"I think we're all here now." Janice's voice carried farther than I would have expected it to. Maybe all shapeshifters' auras exuded past their immediate physical bodies?

As if he were reading my mind, Kade leaned over and said, "She's an elementary school teacher in her day job."

"What is she here?" I whispered.

"On her home turf." At my exasperated glance, he expanded. "Badger. Seriously, don't fuck with her. She's tough."

I watched her as she gathered everyone into the room to take their seats. Someone had brought in dining-table chairs, but many of the twenty or so attendees sat on the floor in postures that seemed oddly informal for something that felt so much like a life-or-death concern.

"Okay, y'all," Janice said. "Settle down. We've got an important issue to discuss tonight."

"Nothing to discuss," a male voice muttered from behind me. "Kill it and be done."

The muscles in my shoulders rippled, and Kade ran a fingertip across the back of my hand. The shock of the delicate stroke distracted me from my own anxiety long enough to allow the shifting urge to pass, at least for the moment.

"That is one possibility, Hank," Janice said, but her tone reminded me of my mother's when she was leading a student to a different conclusion altogether. "But we need to consider all our options here." She turned toward my place on the couch. "Toward that end, Kade Nevala has asked to address the Council." With a wave of her hand, she ceded the floor to the mongoose shifter.

Kade's hand trailed across mine as he stood up, a final supportive gesture before he moved away from me.

I hadn't realized quite how much comfort I had been drawing from the physical connection until he stepped away. Cold air rushed in, and I steeled myself not to shiver again. Instinct told me that would be taken as weakness in this crowd. Taking a deep breath, I sat up straight and tried to look respectable.

When Kade reached the open center of the room, he

took a moment to scan the faces around him, assessing, nodding to a few, sliding his eyes past others.

"You all know why we're here tonight," he said. "Both reasons." With a jerk of his chin, he indicated me. My spine tingled, but I didn't move, didn't take my eyes off of Kade, whose own golden gaze held mine steadily for a few seconds. "First is the discovery of a lamia in Fort Worth. One who has been living here for years, living as a human, under human law and human rules. One who poses absolutely no threat to our community. Lindi Parker has no connection with lamia tradition."

"But—" Someone started to interrupt Kade, maybe Hank from earlier, but the doctor held up a hand and the voice fell silent, another effect of Kade's air of authority. I felt the power pouring out of him, holding everyone in place.

"The second reason, of course, is the death of several shifter children." A low growl rumbled through the room at his words, and might have burst into a full-blown howl if Kade hadn't held the room so completely at that moment. As he met each shifter's eyes, though, the sound died out.

"We all know that the latest child has evidence of a lamia attack. And yes, there does seem to be a connection to Lindi—" Again, he held up a hand for silence. "But it's not the connection you might expect."

I didn't dare look around, though I could feel eyes boring into me, burning into my skin as I kept my own gaze firmly on Kade.

"Lindi Parker is not a danger to us. Lindi is a counselor, a woman who spends her days working with hurt children, helping them heal." His repetition of my name caught my attention, and I wondered if any of the other shifters in the room caught what he was doing. I often used the name-repetition technique in group counseling sessions to make the participants more real to one another, to humanize them.

Though maybe here the word would be *shifterize*.

In any case, in Kade's words, I became not "the lamia," but "Lindi," a person, someone like everyone else in the room.

For an instant, I dared to glance around part of the room. Several of the Council members were leaning forward, nodding. But just as many were leaning away from Kade, and many of those with arms crossed defensively. Charismatic aura or no, Kade Nevala wasn't convincing everyone in the room.

He talked a little longer, extolling my virtues until I almost didn't recognize myself in his words. Was that really how he saw me? Kind, giving, caring, connected to the people around me, from a loving home with wonderful parents. A person with deep ties to the community.

The opposite of what they might think a lamia would be.

Then he dropped his bomb. "Lindi Parker is here tonight to request Council approval for entry into our community."

I was? That was news to me, though not exactly unwelcome. Being part of the shifter world wasn't high on my list of desires, but it might offer protection from whatever was going on. From whoever was really murdering children connected to me.

I just wished Kade had discussed it with me, first.

From the sudden roar of shouts around me, so did the Council members.

Kade held both hands up for silence. When the noise subsided, he turned in a complete circle to catch the eye of every shifter I had identified as disagreeing with him earlier, and a few I had missed. He settled his attention on the Clint Eastwood lookalike slouched in the armchair across from me. Kade's voice grew hard, a buzz of something like anger threading through it. "Make no mistake. This is an official request, which means that until the Council makes its final determination, she is under the Shields' protection."

One corner of the Shield's lip curled up in a cross between amusement and annoyance, but he nodded his acknowledgment of Kade's point. Beside him, Janice looked thoughtful. "That would mean a full background check," she said. "I'm assuming you want a complete intake analysis? That will take at least a month." I couldn't tell whether or not she approved of the ploy, but she wasn't trying to veto it immediately.

"Let the lamia bitch speak for herself," Hank the Heckler said from behind me.

Kade raised his eyebrows at me, and I nodded, rising slowly and making my way to stand next to him. Taking a deep breath, I tested the room. Kade's scent tasted raw, and the heat rolling off of him nearly scorched me. The rest of the room was a boiling wave of emotion, most of it sharp and powerful.

With a conscious effort, I moved into my professional mode. I had talked suicidal teenagers off of literal, actual ledges.

I could do this.

"I know you have no reason to trust me now," I began. "But you will. Dr. Nevala and I will help find the monster that is killing these children. And you'll see that it's not me. I know only a small part of lamia history, but I assure you, I am not what you fear."

"So do you affirm the request for Council-approved membership?" Janice asked. The way she said the words sounded official, almost ceremonial.

"Yes," I replied. "I do."

She nodded. "Then there's nothing further to discuss tonight." When a grumble arose from the back of the room, she growled, baring her teeth. "Not in my house, Hank Cleveland." She waited until he fell silent, then turned to me, her voice neutral—not unkind, but not especially encouraging. "Thank you, Lindi. You have given us quite a bit to discuss. You may go now."

As I navigated my way through the now-silent room, the intensity of emotions flowed through my nose and mouth. A miasma of anger, hate, despair, swirled across the top of my mouth, feeding me information about the Council as I moved among them.

They definitely loathed lamias.

But there was more to it than that.

They were also terrified.

"What was that?" I asked as we made our way to the car.

"A ploy for time." Kade's truck beeped as he unlocked it. He reached around my side and opened the door for me.

"Not that. The sheer terror in that room." Stepping up onto the runner, I swung myself into the passenger side. My voice dropped. "Are they really that afraid of lamias?"

Kade didn't respond until he was buckled into his own seat. Then he tilted his head and considered as he pulled away from the curb. "More afraid that there might be more than one of you, I think."

"How likely is it that we'll gain enough time?" The slight waver in my voice gave away how much the answer meant to me, I feared.

Kade's hand dropped down on mine on the seat for a moment, his body heat again offering comfort, a sense of safety.

How false was that sense?

Staring out into the darkness as Kade drove me home, I wondered if there really were another lamia out there.

If so, what could he or she teach me about my own background?

And how dangerous might it be to find out?

I MANAGED to make it through the next day as if nothing unusual had happened, but only because I was distracted by a batch of new intake cases. I turned off all thoughts of lamias and shapeshifters and concentrated on being merely Lindi Parker, Licensed Professional Counselor. LPCs don't have to worry about being under the protection of Council Shields, or wondering if they might be killed for merely existing—no more than any normal person does, anyway.

I managed to work right through lunch, meeting clients and writing up reports on those meetings.

It was a nice reprieve from the anxiety of the last week.

Too bad it lasted only through the workday.

Moments after five o'clock, my personal phone rang with Scott's ringtone. I was still holding it in my hand, trying to decide whether to answer it, when Kade walked through the door.

"You going to do anything other than stare at that?" he asked.

I bit my lip. "It's Scott. I don't feel up to trying to explain away shifter stuff today. But he might have new information."

"Or he could be calling to reschedule your interrupted date." Kade was doing that neutral-tone thing again, but the golden specks in his eyes were beginning to swirl.

The call switched over to voicemail and I flipped the

ringer over to silent. "If it's important, he'll leave a message." I placed the phone face-down on my desk.

The unmistakably bright scent of satisfaction rolled off of Kade, and I shook my head. "What are you doing here, doctor?"

"I was going to see if you had heard from anyone else on the case." He grinned. "But I see you've been avoiding your phone today."

"Is that why you came over instead of calling?" I turned my attention from him as I began to close out my work for the day, saving a few documents and shutting down my computer.

"Nope. I just wanted to see you." The flavor of satisfaction was fading, replaced with something new—or at least new in my experience with Kade. Hesitation.

Interesting.

I bit the inside of my bottom lip, forcing myself to remain silent as I waited to see where Dr. Mongoose was taking this.

He stared at me for a moment, the increasing churn of the gold in his eyes reflecting some inner agitation. When he eventually spoke, his words gave no indication of what might really be bothering him. "I'm on my way to check in on Kirstie. Would you like to go with me?"

I could play that game, too. If he had something important to say to me, he would eventually come out with it. "Sure. Give me about five minutes to wrap up here. I'll meet you in the lobby."

With a nod, the other shifter left my office, leaving the taste of some low-level anxiety dissipating in the air around me.

～

THE SAME SCENT clung to Kade all the way through the drive to the hospital. I waited for him to say something, to tell me what was bothering him.

When he didn't, I leaned back in the leather seat of his Jeep and stared out the window at the city rolling past me.

At the hospital, Kirstie had been moved from the ICU to her own room, not far from the room where Kade had kissed me the first time. In fact, it might have been the same room. I hadn't paid enough attention the first time to be sure. I'd been too busy pretending not to like it.

Kirstie was awake and alert, chatting with another doctor. When she saw Kade, she brightened. "Hi, Dr. Nevala," she sang out. "How are you?"

He returned her smile. "I'm doing well. As are you, apparently."

The little bobcat-girl—*kit*, I reminded myself—chattered away cheerfully, stopping only long enough to catch her breath occasionally. From the seat beside the bed, Rita Bryant glared at me once, then ignored me.

I didn't hurt your child, I wanted to say. But today was clearly my day for biting my tongue, and I refrained from speaking at all until Kade said his goodbyes and led me back out into the hospital corridor.

"I take it the antivenin worked," I said.

With a nod, Kade began striding toward the elevators. "Better than I had hoped it would, in fact."

Despite his patient's recovery, anxiety still rolled off him. As the doors slid closed behind us, I finally couldn't stand it any longer. "What is bothering you, then?" I demanded. "You've been jittering ever since you walked into my office."

Kade stilled, watching me through narrowed eyes, then nodded as he came to some decision. "You need to begin training."

"Training? To do what?"

"To fight. As a shifter."

I turned my hands palm-up. "What if I don't want to learn to fight? Anyway, why does that have you so agitated?"

"If the Council knew I was training you, they might kill us both."

CHAPTER
SEVENTEEN

"Are you sure no one will see us?" I whispered.

"We're still in the car. You can speak up." Kade's golden eyes laughed at me, though his mouth stayed suspiciously straight.

After he threatened me in the elevator with death-by-Council, I had firmly refused any training he might have to offer. Yet, by the time he dropped me off at my office, he had arranged to pick me up at home an hour after sunset.

I still wasn't sure how that had happened.

Damn mongoose pheromones. Or maybe those golden eyes.

In any case, I went with him when he showed up at my doorstep and got in his Jeep for an hour-long drive to a state park.

"Are you absolutely certain that no one will be out there to catch us shifting?" This time I spoke loudly on purpose.

The mongoose shifter shrugged, his gaze still dancing with amusement. "And say what? Oh, no, there are terrible animal-people in the state park? Anyway, at this time of night, there won't be anyone else around. We all use the park on a pretty regular basis, though we make the wolves do their full-moon runs somewhere else."

"Full-moon run? Is that thing about werewolves and the full moon true?" The rest of his sentence caught up with my brain. "Why do the wolves have to go other places?"

"Slow down. You can't learn everything about us all at once. But no. Werewolves don't have to turn on the full moon any more than you and I do. But they really like to. They can't run at the state park because it's too close to the wildlife park. And the wildlife park is full of various kinds of prey animals—deer, antelope, zebras, mountain goats, and the like. All it takes is one wolf who can't control himself, and the whole pack could go into hunting mode." He rolled his eyes. "Group hunters. They can't seem to help it."

I glanced out at the empty land running by the spot where we had pulled off of Highway 67. "So where do they run?"

This time Kade did grin. "You're not supposed to know."

"But you do?" I examined the end of my ponytail, trying to look uninterested. Cool. Not like I was hanging on every word he said.

"I'm on the Council," he said, his tone matter-of-fact.

I glanced out the window into the darkness, realizing that the conversation had distracted me from my anxiety. "Okay. Your little ploy worked. I'm ready."

Kade's grin flashed again. "Good. Let's go."

We left the truck about a mile from the park entrance. The park was still and silent as we skirted the entrance gate. A light was shining in the guardhouse, but I couldn't sense anyone inside. A little farther down the path, next to the gift-shop, towered two life-size dinosaur replicas.

"What if someone catches us?"

I had gone back to whispering, but Kade answered in his normal tone. "There are people around. The park has campsites and hiking trails. We probably won't see anyone, but even if we run into any Park Rangers, they won't do anything worse than warn us about wandering around at night, tell us to go back to our campsite. Maybe ask to see our permit."

"Which we don't have," I pointed out.

"We can try to hide, if it makes you feel better."

I nodded, and Kade chuckled. "You ever been to Dinosaur Valley before?" he asked as we slipped into the sparse coverage of the foliage by the side of the road leading up to the main parking lot.

"Dad brought me when I was younger to see the dinosaur tracks," I said absently, concentrating on testing the air around us. Flickering my tongue out of my mouth, I drew in the night air. From our left came the taste of the river, the molecules tumbling across my tongue as the water danced through the shallows, then slowing as the river pooled in the deep swimming hole I remembered from my childhood.

We emerged from the trees at the top of the trail that crisscrossed down the slope to the river below.

"What did you think of the place then?" Kade asked, pausing to lean on the rail overlooking the swimming hole. A metal pipe pointed directly at the one fossilized dinosaur track preserved just under the water, allowing viewers to pinpoint the track's location. The reflection of the moonlight on the water didn't provide enough illumination now, but I remembered staring at it intently as a child. Later, I had swum up to the edge of the track's shelf, Dad warning me against adding to erosion by touching it, even as I marveled at the difference between the enormous three-toed track and my tiny hand.

Even in the midst of that awe, part of me had wondered if I was somehow descended from the dinosaurs.

Maybe Kade knew.

Maybe someday I would ask.

"It was impressive," I said simply.

Kade turned and led the way down the path to the river, sure-footed even in the darkness. We passed just above the outcropping with the print, the water low enough that I could see the ancient outline of the print, pressed into mud eons ago, then buried and turned to stone.

Past the swimming hole, the path swung upward again, then took us to manmade stone steps leading down to the river, where we crossed on giant boulders. As a child, Dad had held my hand when we walked across. When Kade reached back to make sure I stayed balanced on one of the slippery rocks, a similar sense of absolute safety encompassed me.

Which was stupid. We were out in the middle of a state park, illegally, in order to hone my fighting skills. "Why did we have to come all the way out here?" I asked once we reached the far bank. "We could have gone out to my parents' ranch. There aren't any park rangers or other people out there."

"You'll see," Kade replied cryptically.

"We're going to shift, right? What if some camper sees us?" I slid into the shadow of a tree leaning out from the bank above me, tempted to scamper from one dark spot to the next.

"Because reports of shapeshifters are always taken so very seriously." Kade peered into the underbrush. "Come on. It's not far now."

We walked close to the water. Reflected moonlight lit the limestone cliffs that rose up on either side of the river, showing their sharply defined layers where the river had cut down into stone over the centuries. Soon, the cliffs petered out, the riverbed widening as the water ran shallower.

"Here," Kade said, turning away from the river and pushing through tangled underbrush and into a dense copse of trees. We emerged on the other side in a small clearing. Striding to the center, Kade closed his eyes and held out his hands, palms down. "There," he breathed. "Feel that?"

"No." I glanced around the empty space. Tall native grasses bounded the area, but nothing grew in the clearing itself. Only light, rocky soil covered the space, about eight feet across. It was so perfectly circular that it looked intentional. And for all I knew, it might be.

I had no idea what Kade meant, but I was willing to give it a try, so I held out my own arms and closed my eyes, trying to feel whatever he meant.

Nothing. I dropped my hands to my sides.

"Try this," Kade said, moving around behind me. Taking my hands in his, he lifted our arms together.

I felt something then. I felt Kade, pressed up against me, the heat of his fingers touching my skin as his breath stirred my hair.

That probably wasn't what he meant, but it was all I could think of at that moment.

When I closed my eyes, I imagined I could feel his heartbeat through our shirts where his chest barely brushed my back as our breathing synchronized.

Wait. That really was his heartbeat.

My eyes flew open, and the sensation disappeared. "What was that?" I asked breathlessly.

Kade dropped my hands and stepped around in front of me again, grinning. "I thought you might be able to sense it. Not all of us can."

"Sense what?" But I didn't really need an answer. Now that Kade had pointed it out, I was attuned to the feeling.

Power.

Thrumming up through the earth at my feet, spilling out into the circle where we stood.

"Where is it coming from?" I asked.

Kade shook his head. "No idea. As far as anyone can tell, it's always been here. There are other spots, too, all over the world, but this is the closest one to us."

"Can we use it somehow?" The sensation intensified, swirling around me.

"Try," Kade said with a smile.

I closed my eyes and held out my hands again, letting the strange energy twine up my body and around my fingers, caressing me as it slid up my face and through my hair.

When I opened my eyes, a white haze shivered in between me and the world.

But when I tried to close my hands around it, the power ran through my fingers like water, dropping back to the ground, leaving me trembling in the night air. "Wow."

"Good. Now call it back and shift," Kade said, watching me intently.

I usually stripped before shifting. But I wasn't about to take off my clothes, not with Kade Nevala watching me like that. The thought brought my nipples to attention, though, and Kade tilted his head, narrowing his eyes at me thoughtfully.

I told myself it was the magic of this place, even though I knew better.

Shifting in my clothes, then. I'd done it before. I ignored the fact that most of the time, it left half of what I was wearing ripped and torn.

Naked now, or torn garments later?

Turning my back on the were-mongoose, I pulled my shirt over my head, pretending I didn't feel him watching every move. When my panties and bra were neatly folded on the stack of clothing on the ground, I prepared to shift.

Closing my eyes, I concentrated on pulling that throbbing energy back around me. When it encircled me entirely, I drew my arms down to my sides slowly, allowing the twitch of muscle to become a ripple that ran through my back and out to my entire body.

I opened my eyes when I felt them begin to shift. Something about seeing the change from color vision to black-and-white always made the transformation move more quickly. Once my eyes had shifted entirely, the haze turned to a light sheen with thousands of sparkling lights dancing within it.

I dropped down to the ground as my arms and legs flowed into one long, muscular body, and for the first time ever, I didn't feel panic.

For the first time, the shift felt right. Natural.

The sparkles faded from my eyes, though I could still feel the thrumming magic in the ground below me.

I reared up to watch Kade as he, too, shifted, and realized that this was the first time I'd seen him in his mongoose form.

He had undressed as I shifted, and I had just a glimpse of his muscular human shape before he, too, pulled the magic around him and began to shift.

Watching it from outside, I could see the way the tiny, star-bright motes of light flew not just around the shapeshifter, but through him, sparking changes everywhere they touched. When the twinkling lights faded, Kade the mongoose stood in front of me.

I've always thought that the word "mongoose" was silly.

The animal in front of me was anything but.

He looked fierce.

The golden-brown color of his fur matched the color of his human eyes. In his animal form, those eyes were darker, but still swirled with golden flecks. His body was compact, lean, muscular, again much like his human shape.

I found myself sizing him up as an adversary. His ears were squared off, close to his head, leaving no points to grab.

And then he moved. Flashing toward me, he raised one paw, struck the side of my head, and was gone. Instinctively, I struck out toward him, only to find that he had danced away.

Damn, he was fast.

We spun around again, striking at one another. Kade didn't touch me again, but I didn't touch him, either.

And then he pulled on the magic in that circle. I saw it happen, saw the glittering lights begin to sparkle around him, but I didn't know what he was doing until those twinkles became one long smear of light and he was pinning me down to the ground, one paw on my head, the other on my back. I thrashed and pulled, but the magic apparently granted strength as well as speed. Kade held me there easily.

Not until I went entirely limp did he let go of the extra power. I saw it drain out of him and back into the ground below us. If this had been a true fight, I would have attacked then. Instead, I simply pulled back and watched as Kade withdrew his paws carefully and jumped away.

It wasn't until he was already mid-shift that I realized that when I retook human form, I would be standing in front of him without any clothes.

My snake-brain didn't care, but some part of my human self whimpered in the back of my mind.

Nothing to be done about it, though.

It wasn't like he wasn't standing in front of me in his human form now, perfectly naked.

And oh, I did mean perfect.

When the sparkles from my own transformation cleared, they didn't drain away immediately. Instead, I stood in the center of a circle of power throbbing around me. The moonlight glinted off the remaining flickers of light, like magical dust motes dancing in the air. I found that by concentrating, I could pull them in and through me, sliding across my skin and then sinking into my body until they infused me with their extra power. When I glanced down at my arms, they glittered with it.

I was so entranced with the sensations that it took me a long moment to realize that Kade was watching me, his churning golden eyes shining through the white haze that now surrounded me.

He hadn't dressed while I shifted, and I had to focus to keep my gaze on his face, rather than allowing it to drift lower.

His slight grin suggested that he knew exactly what I was doing, but he didn't say anything, so I didn't, either.

Then he began to change forms again, and I realized that the exhaustion I usually felt after rapid shifting was missing entirely.

That spicy smell I associated with Kade—half mesmerizing, half terrifying—intensified as his human body almost melted away, dropping him onto all fours, the shimmer enclosing him and twisting the very air around us.

The wave of power accompanying his shift sucked the air out of my lungs.

When the sparkles cleared and I could breathe again, Kade stood in front of me in his mongoose shape, somewhat bigger than the ones I'd seen online, if my sense of scale could be trusted. Then again, it was possible that, as with his human shape, Kade simply exuded power past his actual size.

In any case, it set off every internal warning I had—all my instincts were screaming at me to fight or run.

The bitter taste of adrenaline flooded my mouth and my senses sharpened.

Seconds later, I felt my own shift begin, my body forcing me to take the shape it instinctively knew was best for fighting.

With a deep breath, I pulled the shift back, keeping my arms and legs clearly separated. Still, my vision grayed out —no matter how hard I concentrated, I couldn't keep my eyes human in the face of Kade's mongoose form.

The white sparkles coalesced around the mongoose in front of me and began to fade.

"Now you." Kade's voice echoed through the shimmer circling around him. "But I want you to try a new shape this time."

I had to focus to keep my teeth from sliding into fangs, to be able to use my human voice. "New? I'm a snake shifter. I shift into a snake. Period."

"But I'd guess it's the same snake shape every time, right?" Kade dropped the magic around him, and the glow faded, leaving only afterimages burned into my eyes.

Warily, I nodded.

"You're not just a snake shifter. You're a lamia. You can take any serpent shape you want."

I couldn't see his face any longer, but my gaze must have reflected my skepticism.

"How well do you know snakes?" he asked.

I laughed. "My father is a herpetologist. There's not much I don't know about snakes."

"What's your go-to form?"

"Something close to a cobra."

"Then I want you to try for something different, like a constrictor."

"You know your snakes, too."

"I'm a mongoose. I have to. It was part of my training from early on."

"What do I do?" I continued to carefully keep my eyes focused on his face. *Whatever you do, don't look down.*

"Pull at the Earth magic as you shift again." He seemed utterly unconcerned about his own nakedness.

"And then what?"

"Concentrate. Try pulling the Earth magic deep inside. Hold the shape in your mind as you shift."

"I don't think I can." My shapeshifting wasn't conscious, not really. I didn't imagine myself into my snake shape. I just *changed*.

Even the ability to hold back the change was something I'd had to learn as a child, and it hadn't come easily. Only the fear of shifting in the middle of a school day, combined with a desire to socialize with other children, had finally worked to allow me to maintain my human form under stress.

Except, apparently, the stress of dealing with a certain mongoose shifter.

"You can do this." Kade's voice was soft and insistent. "Hold the form in your mind. Then be the shape you need."

Suzy. An image of her comforting bulk flashed through my mind.

"Python," I said aloud.

Kade nodded approvingly. "Good choice."

I pictured Suzy, imagined her length stretched out before me, first in full-color human vision, then, as I initiated the shift, in the shades of gray that characterized my serpentine sight.

Kade's voice came to me as if from a distance, echoing off ear bones already beginning to change and through the scales covering my head. "Now. Find the Earth magic. Feel it surround you. Let it move through you. Bring it into you."

Once again, I let the power of the place slide into me, flickering through my skin. I worked to pull even more of it through every pore, until it ignited an answering spark inside me. In that moment, I burned, hotter than any reptile ever could—a heat that flashed from one end of my body to the other. If I could have screamed, I would have. But when it was over, the shift was complete and I stretched across the ground, my serpent shape longer and stronger than usual.

I twirled around on myself and saw, in shades of gray, a typical python pattern across my back.

It worked.

Stretching out my entire length, I reveled in the feel of my body, the strength of this shift. Why hadn't I ever known I could shift to more than one form?

The answer came to me instantly: because no one had been around to teach me.

Whatever had happened to my parents—whether they had abandoned me on purpose, or I had wandered away, or they had been killed by someone like Kade and I had simply been missed—the end result had been that I was left without a shapeshifting mentor.

Although a small part of me resented that, and may have even resented Kade for the role his people had played in the near-extinction of the lamias, I also had to admit that with their training, I would almost certainly have become a cold-blooded killer.

The total opposite of what I'd become: a nurturer and a protector for kids who needed me.

As it was, almost no one knew how much I had to

repress that side of myself. Virtually every time I had to work with a child abuser and he (for it was almost always a man) began attempting to justify his actions, I found myself drifting into daydreams of forcing him to endure exactly those things he had inflicted on his victims.

I knew that most abusers had themselves been abused. In that moment, I never cared.

And the desire was even more difficult to shake off in my serpent form.

Up until now, though, that form wouldn't have been useful against human males. It was too small, too powerless.

But as a python—a large one, at that—I would be able to take on those men.

Kade's voice interrupted my spiraling thoughts. "Now, without shifting back to your human form, I want you to take another shape."

I tilted my head at him inquisitively and darted my tongue out into the air.

He certainly smelled serious–and more dangerous than he did when I was a human. Less enticing.

Pulling my attention back to the shift at hand, I considered my options. I wasn't certain I could even do this.

Maybe another constrictor?

As if he were reading my thoughts, Kade said, "And this time, I want you to take a hybrid form. We'll start with a hybrid snake. Maybe a combination of a viper and a constrictor? That should be sufficiently complicated." He barked a short laugh, a sound that I suspected sounded like this mongoose form. "We can put off a human/snake hybrid for another night."

Right. As if this wasn't going to be enough.

I couldn't close my eyes to concentrate as I pulled up

the Earth magic this time. So I simply focused on the tiny glimmers in the air.

What would I want to keep of each form?

How could I mix viper and constrictor?

The answer came to me instantly. Viper's head. Constrictor's body.

I concentrated on the form of a pit viper's head, on changing only that part of my body.

Cobra.

Triangular head. Top fangs, a venom reservoir. Flaring hood.

Pythons already had heat-sensing pits, but as I shifted, they coalesced into one deeper pit on each side of my head, growing even more sensitive with the addition of a heat-sensing membrane.

It was like shifting to ultraviolet vision. I could sense Kade's body heat before. But now, every part of him was lit up, bouncing off my senses like a beacon, every inch radiating information to me.

As my form finished shifting, I pulled the upper third of my body up and flared my hood, weaving back and forth in front of Kade.

The mongoose shifter took an unconscious step back, then forced himself to stop. His golden eyes began to churn in a way I had only seen when he kissed me, and his body heat spiked as he worked to keep from shifting, too.

I hadn't understood why the lamias had been such formidable enemies—not really. Not against werewolves, or large-mammal shifters.

But now? I got it.

I was a twenty-foot long serpent with the muscular strength of a python and the venomous capacity of a cobra of equal size.

Those child molesters I daydreamed about hurting wouldn't have a chance.

And neither would the other shapeshifters, if I ever decided to take them on.

I was more powerful than I had ever realized.

EIGHTEEN

By the time we left the park, I had taken on three other hybrid snake shapes and was equal parts starving and exhausted.

Once again in my human form, I slumped against the headrest in the passenger seat.

"Food first," Kade announced, glancing over at me. "Then rest."

The next thing I knew, the smell of hamburgers drew me out of a deep sleep just as Kade turned the Jeep back onto the highway.

"Here. These are yours." He handed one of several paper sacks to me, and I pulled out a stack of cheeseburgers.

Shifting always left me ravenous. Apparently that was true of other shifters, as well. We ate without speaking, Kade using one hand to drive and the other to steadily consume burgers until there was nothing left but wrappers in the paper sacks.

With my stomach full, I leaned my temple against the window glass and stared up at the stars in the sky, wondering how I might actually use the hybrid forms I had just learned.

"Can all shifters take on more than one animal form?" I didn't take my eyes off the sky.

"No. Most of us can learn to control size to some degree, and almost all of us can manage a human/animal hybrid. But I don't know of any shifters other than lamias who can take on multiple forms of a single animal." Kade's voice was matter of fact, but his words sent a shiver up my spine.

"So I'm still different from all of you?"

I could almost feel the displaced air from Kade's shrug. "We're all different. The first thing I learned in my training to treat shifters is that werewolf biology is different from bobcat shifter biology, and those are both different from mongoose shifter."

"But it is biology? Whatever makes us shift, I mean. It's not magic."

Kade's sharp laugh carried more than a hint of surprise. "Now you're getting into theology. I would say yes. Even in our world, everything comes down to science. But I know that some people would disagree with me. Eduardo Valencia, the Shield we saw at the Council meeting? He calls the place we just left the Holy Circle."

"You called that power *Earth magic*," I pointed out.

"I don't have a better name for it. I might as easily have called it *geologic energy*. I could change terms, if you prefer."

"No." My eyelids were tugging down again. "Just trying to figure all of this out."

Kade's gentle voice came to me as if from far away as I drifted off again. "It's life, Lindi. There's nothing to figure out. You just live it."

When Kade woke me up to tell me we had reached my apartment, those words were still ringing in my ears.

It's life ... you just live it.

It wasn't a philosophy I had lived by. Both my adoptive parents were scientists. They had taught me to question everything. Add to that curiosity a need to obsessively control my actions, or risk giving away the biggest secret I'd ever known, and I had been left with a tendency to analyze everything. Maybe even over-analyze.

I didn't do spontaneous.

Until now.

When the doctor walked me to my door, I unlocked it, then turned and took a single step toward him.

He froze at the movement, but it was the stillness of one predator sizing up another.

The wave of spicy heat rolling off him told me everything I needed to know about his own desires. Without a word, I wrapped my arms around his neck.

Bending down, he brushed his lips against mine, the heat of the contact nearly searing in its intensity.

Sweeping his hands down my back and under my thighs, he lifted me up until I could wrap my legs around his waist. Then he held me with one hand while he pushed the door open. Kicking it shut behind us, he carried me easily down the hall, his tongue darting in and out of my mouth, filling me with the burning heat of him.

Shifting energy rolled up my back, and I could feel the skin along my spine shift from serpentine to human, back and forth, shivering from my neck down to the base of my back. The sensation pushed me forward, crushing me against Kade's chest, pulling a whimper from deep in my throat.

An answering growl rose from Kade, and at the same moment I heard the sound of tearing cloth, I felt the mongoose shifter barely avoid puncturing my skin with the claws he'd just sprung.

I tightened my legs more firmly around him, felt his

erection press against me as his breathing grew more ragged.

I pulled away long enough to point. "That way. "

At the end of the hall, I fumbled for the doorknob and Kade pushed my bedroom door open with his booted foot and slid us onto the bed without breaking the kiss. The shapes of his fingers more under his own control, he gently pulled my t-shirt off, then deftly unhooked the black cotton bra I'd worn underneath—some part of my mind determined to ignore the attraction between us, insisting that if I wore my plainest underwear, I wouldn't end up in bed with him.

Yeah, right.

From frantic kisses, Kade slowed to deliberate movements, sliding the straps off my shoulders and placing soft, hot kisses everywhere they touched.

When my bra hit the floor, I sat up and tugged at the bottom of Kade's own shirt, adding first it and then his jeans to the growing pile at the foot of my bed.

This time, when we both ended up naked, I stared my fill, then ran my hand along the hard planes of Kade's stomach. Then his mouth was everywhere, and I could no longer think clearly. When he entered me, so much heat surrounded us that I worried for a moment about spontaneous combustion. As we moved together, the air around us shimmered, red-hot sparks shining in my eyes, reminiscent of the cooler, white diamond sparkles of Earth magic in Kade's Holy Circle.

The last few moments were a blur of scales and fur, the two of us only barely holding on to our basic human shapes, and only out of the most primitive of needs, until the heat from our joining exploded into something exquisite, both of us crying out within moments of one another.

Afterwards, we slept in a tangle of arms and legs, once again fully human, but still unwilling to completely disengage from one another.

At some point in the early hours of the morning, I heard Kade whisper, "I've got to go to the hospital. I'll see you soon."

Part of me worried that we needed to talk about what had happened—but the rest of me decided it could wait.

As it turned out, that was the wrong decision.

CHAPTER
NINETEEN

The next day felt much longer than it really was.

I didn't know how long Kade and I had spent out in the state park, or what time we had gotten home—or for that matter, how much time we had spent in that half-magical shifter-sex trance—but I knew for certain that I hadn't gotten enough rest.

It was difficult to believe it had been such a short time since the first night I had met Kade. I didn't go around kissing strange men, and I didn't hop into bed with them, either.

And yet that was almost exactly what I had done.

I hadn't even met with Emma Camelli yet—the young shifter who had killed her molesting stepfather.

I had left a message with her mother the day after the attack, but had been too distracted by the shapeshifter events in my own life since then to do any further follow-up.

To be honest, I hadn't thought of her much at all, assuming that Moreland would give me a call once everything was lined up for her case.

She might be a shapeshifter, but surely we could follow standard intake procedures, right?

All I wanted to do now was get home and go to bed, sleep for a year or two before I had to deal with anything else. I knew that was a futile dream the instant I heard Emma Camelli's whisper on my voicemail. "Please come help me. Someone is trying to kill me. Someone like you."

Icy fear poured down along my spine as I stared at the number recorded on the screen. I didn't recognize it, couldn't tell if she had called me from her home phone or a cell.

I had a reverse-number program on my office computer. I could find it that way.

I could also call the police, or even Scott.

But bringing them in to search for *someone like me* might mean exposing the shapeshifter community, and although no one had said as much, I suspected that the Council wouldn't react well to that.

I considered my options as I unlocked the CAP-C building and, once in my office, turned on the computer.

What if I did contact the police and we found Emma in her shifter shape? I hadn't gotten a clear description from her, but what she had described using as she killed her stepfather sounded suspiciously like a limb covered by a kind of carapace. If I was right, Emma was some sort of insectoid shifter. How might the human world react to that?

No. I had to turn to the shifters for help with this.

But Kade was the only shifter I knew how to contact by phone, and when I dialed, he didn't answer.

Dammit. Was he ignoring me?

Fear bloomed in my stomach. Was there something worse going on?

I dialed again, even as I pulled up the reverse-number

search engine and typed in the number Emma had called from.

A cell phone, registered to Emma's mother.

I hadn't met the woman yet—their follow-up appointment with me wasn't scheduled until next week —but I knew where they were staying while they waited for the crime scene in their home to be released by the police.

Still no answer from Kade.

Maybe he was dealing with an emergency at the hospital?

Shutting down the computer, I left the office and strode quickly to my car. As I started the engine, I tapped in a text message to the mongoose shifter: *Emma Camelli in danger. Going to check on her.* And then I added the name of the hotel Emma's mother had given the CAP-C receptionist when she called. Finally, I called one last time and left the same information in a voicemail.

The hotel wasn't terribly far from my office. If Emma was there and simply panicked, then this would be a quick trip.

If she wasn't there, I would have to figure out what to do next.

And if she's not alone there?

I hushed the voice in the back of my head. If she wasn't alone—if there was another lamia there—I would take on the fighting shape Kade had taught me earlier.

No matter how exhausted I might be.

On the way over to the hotel, I told myself that I would keep my phone with me. I could call Moreland if things looked sketchy.

But when I got there, the whole place looked risky. The sun had just dropped below the horizon, and the purpling twilight made the whole area, poorly maintained at the best of times, look like it had been bombed out and abandoned at some point in the recent past.

I drove my car around behind the motel, pulling to the far side of the lot to park. I stepped out and stood there uncertainly, one hand resting on the still-open car door, the other holding my phone.

Emma's room was on the second floor. I couldn't tell anything from out here. The windows were all featureless and blank, showing nothing but the stained white waves of the vinyl blackout curtains.

"This is stupid, Lindi," I muttered to myself. Not to mention dangerous.

Without taking my eyes off the motel rooms, I moved around to the trunk and dug out a tire iron.

It was the closest thing I had to a weapon—other than myself. I didn't want to shift unless I absolutely had to.

Scrolling through my contacts, I found Moreland's number, and dialed. I was in the middle of leaving him a message when I heard Emma scream. The sound spurred me into motion. As I dashed across the lot and up the concrete and metal stairs, I hissed into the phone, "Something's happening. Hurry!"

Without bothering to thumb it off, I dropped the phone into the pocket of my pants. If I had to shift, I wanted to know where to find it afterwards.

I slowed as I drew closer to the room.

The smartest thing to do would be shift before I tried to burst in. But that would leave me exposed to anyone who happened to walk by, or even look out a window.

Not to mention the difficulty not having hands might cause when it came to breaking into a hotel room.

Okay, then.

Break in first.

Shift later—if possible, or even necessary.

I stopped long enough to check the doorknob, just in case the door was unlocked. When it wasn't, I lifted the tire iron behind my head and closed my eyes to draw on the power I knew I could use to shift.

It wasn't the Earth magic of the Holy Circle, but it was something powerful, all the same. With a deep breath, I pushed at that energy, shoving it down through my arms in one mighty wave even as I swung the bar I held.

With an enormous crunch, the window spider-webbed, cracks crawling across the glass. A second, concentrated swing sent it spraying inward in a shower that I hoped didn't injure Emma.

I took a step to one side and used the crowbar to pull the curtain back.

After the huge crashing noise, I half-expected a manager to round the corner at full-speed. Instead, the entire motel complex seemed even quieter than before, if that was possible.

I could see only a small portion of the room from my place beside the window, and from what I could tell, it was empty. As slowly as possible, I tugged the blackout curtain back farther, and took a quick peek inside before ducking back against the outside wall.

Standard low-rent hotel room. King bed, dresser, bathroom vanity against the far wall.

And I swear I had caught a glimpse of the tail-end of a snake slithering into the tiny enclosure with the shower and toilet.

More importantly, though, were the forms on the bed— at least three of them, all too small to be adults.

All human, at least at the moment, one of them with dishwater blonde hair that I was certain belonged to Emma Camelli.

If that had really been a snake slithering into the bathroom, did that mean these children had been taken by another lamia?

I almost couldn't decide if I wanted to believe that there were other lamias out in the world, or to hope that my eyes had been playing tricks on me.

Almost.

Another, longer look into the room suggested that the way in was clear, at least for the moment. Draping curtain fabric over my arm to protect it from any remaining glass shards, I reached around and popped open the lock.

The door opened without any trouble, though I'd been half afraid someone would be waiting behind it. At the noise, though, one of the forms on the bed began whimpering.

"It's okay," I whispered. "I'm here to help."

I used the crowbar to do a quick check under the bed-ruffle.

Nothing but a board blocking guests from losing anything there.

All of the bodies on the bed were young girls, ranging from about six to ten, and there were four of them, not three. They all watched me, but none of them moved.

What had been used to subdue them? Keeping one eye on that bathroom door, now closed, I quickly pulled the coverlet back far enough to get a look at the girls.

No restraints.

Drugs, then.

No clothes, either.

I could think about what else might have been done to them later, after we were all safe.

"Everything is going to be okay," I repeated. "I'm here to save you." It hardly mattered what I said, as long as I kept talking, kept reassuring them. "Emma called me to come get you. I'm going to put this cover back over you to keep you warm. No one else will hurt you."

Flicking my tongue out, I tasted the air around me. At least two of the girls were mammals of some sort, and the scent of their fear permeated the room. Under that, though, I could taste other scents. A bird of some sort, presumably one of the girls. Something insectoid—whatever Emma was. Fainter than that, humans, people who had come in and out of the room over the last days and weeks. And interweaved with all the other smells, just the tiniest hint of something familiar. Something serpentine.

Another lamia had been here, sometime fairly recently.

Emma whimpered, pulling my attention back to the girls on the bed.

The youngest, a tiny brunette with dark brown eyes, watched me intently, tears leaking out from under her eyelids. The others alternately watched me and glanced wildly at the bathroom door.

I nodded toward the bathroom to let them know I understood. "I know. It's all okay. The police are coming, too."

I hoped that was true. I had left enough messages, anyway.

A rustling noise—maybe the shower curtain?—drew my entire attention toward the back of the room. I hefted the tire iron up like a baseball bat and tiptoed toward the closed door. The flicker of tail I'd seen disappearing hadn't looked like it belonged to an especially large snake. Probably no bigger than my own cobra shape. The vanity was outside the bathroom, leaving little space for anyone inside to shift to a larger shape.

That's what I hoped, anyway.

Slowly, I placed my left hand on the knob, hefting the metal bar in the right.

I could do this. I had to do this. I couldn't just wait for someone else to show up and take care of the problem.

The possibility that the Council might do terrible things to humans who discovered shapeshifters flitted through my mind, and I dismissed it for later consideration.

I took a deep breath and began turning the knob.

"Freeze!" The deep voice came from outside the door, and I jumped in surprise, letting go of the unopened knob.

"Drop the tire iron." I peered in the mirror, but I couldn't see anything but a vague figure outside the room —only his hands and gun were clearly visible.

The iron clattered to the floor, and I put both hands in the air, remaining perfectly still, until Scott Carson entered the room, holding a gun on me.

When he made eye contact in the mirror, he blinked, pulling his finger off the trigger and pointing the barrel of his weapon straight into the air.

"Dammit, Lindi," he breathed. "What are you doing here? You could've gotten hurt."

Crap. Of all the people who could have shown up, why did it have to be Scott? I might have been able to get Moreland to help me—might have even been able to tell him about the shifters and trusted him to keep it a secret.

Could I trust Scott with my deepest secret? I couldn't very well let him go into that bathroom blind.

"I think I heard something in there," I finally said, gesturing toward the closed door as I stepped away.

"Something or someone?"

I shrugged. "Just a noise."

With a nod, he waved me back out of the way. "Go stay with the girls."

I was impressed. He'd barely glanced at the bed in the room before identifying the victims. Moving to the bed, I perched on the edge, murmuring to the children still immobilized there. "It'll be okay. Mr. Carson is an investigator with the District Attorney's office."

Scott pounded on the door, and I jerked. One of the girls on the bed also twitched. I hoped that was a good sign that whatever drugs had been used were wearing off.

"District Attorney's Investigator," he barked. "Open up." He waited about ten seconds, and then he turned the knob, pushed the door open, and followed his gun in.

I assumed that Scott had called backup, but just in case, I pulled my phone out and dialed 911. It was better than jittering.

From my seat on the bed I couldn't see anything but the blue oxford-cloth shirt that covered his back. There was a little movement, and I heard the shower curtain rings scrape across their pole. Not long after, Scott came out of the bathroom.

"Empty," he said shortly.

"What?" I popped to my feet. "That's impossible. Someone went in there, I know it. The door was open, and then it closed right as I came in."

The investigator held up his hands. "I believe you. There's a window in there. It's been opened."

I headed toward the bathroom to see for myself, but Scott put out an arm to stop me. "We don't want to contaminate the scene any more than absolutely necessary."

I nodded, but also gritted my teeth. I wanted to see if I could scent anything that he might have missed. But I couldn't very well say that aloud.

A tinny voice floated up to me, and I realized that the 911 operator had been speaking for several seconds, trying to get a response while the phone dangled uselessly in my hands.

"Here," I said, handing it to Scott. "I called 911. You talk to them. I'm going to see what I can do for the girls."

Finally convinced that it was safe to truly care for the victims in the room, I moved back to the bed.

"Don't move them," Scott warned.

I flashed a look at him. "I know how to deal with trauma victims. It's in my job description. I'm just going to talk to them until the ambulance gets here."

"Sorry. Habit." He smiled at me, then began pacing around the room, carefully examining every detail as he spoke to the operator, giving her his information and requesting ambulances and squad cars.

"Get them to send Moreland, too," I requested. Scott waved over his shoulder at me as he peered into the bathroom again.

When he came back into the main part of the room, he handed the phone to me again, and his fingers brushed against mine. For the first time ever, physical contact with Scott sent a shiver down my back—not unlike the response I'd had to Kade the night before.

We both froze, staring at one another.

What was that?

In the distance, I heard sirens wailing, drawing my attention away from Scott just long enough for him to pull away and the spell of the moment to be broken.

MORELAND ARRIVED WITH THE AMBULANCES. The EMTs took over working with the girls, placing IVs in their arms and running fluid into them in hopes of flushing the drugs through their systems more quickly, and at that point I was able to begin moving back toward the bathroom. Eventually, I was able to slide around the door when no one else was looking. I was careful not to touch anything, but I focused on carefully shifting only the inside of my mouth—

and only enough so I could better tell exactly what had gone through the window.

Once I had my Jacobson's gland in place, I flickered my tongue out and pulled in the air around me.

Much better than trying to do this with my human mouth.

This way, I could parse every molecule, take it apart to learn what it held.

Humans. Lots of humans, their flavors piled on top of one another, meaty and hot.

The humid remainder of a soapy shower—recent, maybe even after the girls were taken.

Scott. More of him than I would have expected, given the short amount of time he was in here.

I shook my head.

None of that was what I needed.

Leaning over the edge of the tub, I flicked my tongue out toward the window, noting with my human eyes the rusted and broken bars that had once protected it.

There.

From the edge of the windowsill, I caught a whiff of the scent I sought. Serpentine. Female. And not like anything I'd ever come across before—not outside of my own home, anyway.

Lamia.

With that confirmation, I started to turn away, but at the last moment, a slight flutter caught my eye.

I leaned closer, peering down at it.

Snakeskin?

As if the lamia had been shedding as she worked her way out of the bathroom?

That was odd.

Shedding was the one snake-like thing I had never

done, and Dad had speculated that something about my human blood made it impossible.

Moving quickly, I plucked the tiny scrap of skin off the rusted metal where it had caught and slipped it into my pocket. I didn't know what it could tell me, but I knew that I didn't want anyone else to have it.

I was still focusing on shifting my mouth back to its human form when Moreland came in behind me, his tall, bulky form making the bathroom feel even smaller.

"Find anything interesting in here?" he asked.

When I turned and met his gaze, he was staring at me through suspicious green eyes.

"Nope. Didn't touch anything, either." I gestured toward the window. "But I don't know how anyone could have gotten out of there."

Moreland leaned forward to peer at the broken bars. "Have to be someone pretty small," he agreed. "Maybe they pushed the bars back into place?" He shook his head. "No telling. Adrenaline will let people do some wild shit. Probably freaked out when they heard you come in."

I made a noncommittal noise.

"Anyway," the detective continued. "Your doctor friend is here. He says you called him?"

My cheeks flared scarlet. "I couldn't reach anyone else. I thought someone should know where I went."

"You didn't think calling me and Scott Carson would be enough?"

"I didn't call Scott." I paused. "I thought you did."

"Detective Moreland," one of the EMTs called from across the room. "We're leaving, taking the girls over to Kindred."

I followed Moreland out into the room, where Kade was in full-on doctor-mode, conferring with one of the other EMTs.

"Hey," he said when he caught sight of me. "You okay?"

"Yeah. But I'd like to see you take care of the girls." I tried to convey that I had something important to tell him with nothing more than my eyes. I'm not sure I managed it, but he seemed to know what I was trying to tell him, anyway.

"Follow us over to the hospital, then?"

"I'd like to ask Lindi a few questions first," Moreland interjected.

"I'll meet you over there when I'm done," I suggested.

Kade nodded, already half-distracted by his job, and waved once before following the four stretchers out of the motel room and down the stairs. Scott, who had been talking to one of the uniformed officers, followed with a short wave toward Moreland and me.

Moreland's questions didn't take long—he walked me through the events of the evening, starting with Emma's phone message. I told him everything with the exception of seeing the tail-end of the lamia sliding into the bathroom and finding the scrap of skin caught on the window.

"Why didn't you call 911 from the beginning?" he asked. "Or the station? They could have sent a car over."

"I didn't want to overreact." I held up both hands to ward off any complaint. "I know, I know. I should have done more. I really do know better."

"This isn't your standard molestation case," he reminded me. "Someone is killing these kids. I don't want any more victims—and I sure as hell don't want you to end up in my case files."

"I'm sorry, Daniel." I placed one hand lightly on his forearm. "I promise it won't happen again."

He narrowed those green eyes at me and searched my own gaze, then nodded. "Okay. Go ahead and get over to the hospital. See what you can find out. I'll be over as soon as the Crime Scene Unit guys are done here. Don't wait on me, though. It could take a while. We can catch up tomorrow if we need to."

I hadn't realized how unsteady I was until I began to walk down the stairs—the entire evening's events had made me more anxious than I realized. But I had worked hard to earn the trust and respect of the men on Moreland's team. I wasn't about to let them see me get shaky. So I held it together until I got to my car, started it, and drove down the street.

Then I pulled over and shook for a solid ten minutes.

It was a shocky reaction—I knew that from my experience working with other people who had survived a traumatic event.

I was also starving, almost as hungry as I'd been the night before, when all I had done tonight was shift my mouth.

Whatever the cause, I decided it was more important to get food than to get to the hospital quickly. After I'd gone through a drive-through and scarfed down four hamburgers, I felt like I might survive.

By the time I walked into the hospital, I was feeling almost like myself again.

Almost cheerful, given the circumstances.

After all, I had helped save four young shapeshifters from a horrific death.

I was stunned when Kade, coming around a corner and seeing me walking alone down a momentarily empty hall, grabbed me by the arm and slung me into the nearest empty room.

Slamming the door behind us, he shoved me against the nearest wall, his forearm pressed against my chest to hold me into place. The vanilla milkshake I had been sipping on my way to the nurses' station flew out of my hand and landed on the floor, spraying out across the tile.

I let out an inarticulate cry. Kade responded by pushing against me even harder.

"What the hell did you think you were doing tonight?" he demanded.

CHAPTER
TWENTY

I shoved back against his arm, but Kade kept me pinned to the wall.

I might not be able to make him get off me, but I could sure as hell respond verbally. "What do you mean, what was I doing?"

"Do you have any idea how much trouble you could have gotten into?" He leaned into my face, the anger rolling off him like steam, heating up the entire room. "Bad enough you could have gotten yourself killed. But you could have exposed us all—the entire shifter community." By this point, he was virtually spitting the words out into my face.

Again, I tried to push against his arm. The fiery emotion surrounding us made my back pop and roll. I forced the shift back down, and saw Kade gritting his teeth to do the same.

"Isn't that why you had some guy watching me all the time?" I demanded as soon as I had control of myself. "Where's the Council's precious Shield? Why didn't he show up to help? If it's so important to keep the shapeshifter community safe, why was I there all alone?" If we had been entirely alone, the last words would have come out in a shout. As it was, we were both hissing, spitting our accusations into one another's faces.

Kade slumped, all of the anger suddenly draining out of him. He blew out a breath, lifted his arm away from me, held his hands up in a sign of surrender, and took a step back.

"I don't know," he said. "And it's got me worried."

I was still too angry—too shocked and hurt by Kade's actions and accusations—to drop my defenses.

"Then I think you should figure it out." I stepped away from the wall, brushed my hands over the spot Kade had pressed against to smooth my shirt down, and moved toward the door. "Are the girls I saved able to communicate yet?" I emphasized the words *I saved*.

"They're beginning to." Kade watched me warily, but he didn't take another step toward me. "I expect them to be fully recovered tomorrow, at least physically."

"I'll be by tomorrow to interview them." I put one hand on the door handle, then paused and spoke over my shoulder. "And Kade? If you ever shove me into another room— or touch me in any way without my permission—you'll be sorry."

I didn't know exactly what I thought I would do to the were-mongoose if he did attack me, but the sound of the vague threat pleased me as I stalked out of the room and let the door slam.

I was still contemplating the possibilities when I rounded the corner toward the front entrance and almost bumped into Scott.

"Hey," the investigator said, running a hand through his dark hair. "You talked to the vics yet?"

"No." I tried to avoid thinking about my exchange with Kade. I needed to concentrate on what I said to Scott—it would be too easy to give too much away if I didn't pay attention. "Whatever the kidnapper gave them is only now starting to wear off."

The hand in his hair moved down to wipe across his eyes. "So that can wait until tomorrow," he said. "Good." He spun on his heel and fell into step with me back toward the entrance.

"Yeah. I should go back to the office and write up a report, but I don't think I'm up to it." A tiny laugh escaped me. "Actually, that might be an understatement."

Scott's mouth twisted in a wry grin. "It's been a hell of a night." He paused as if considering, then took a breath and plunged ahead. "You want to call it a night as far as work is concerned? Maybe go grab a beer or something?"

I hesitated. So far our outings had been limited to lunch and that one aborted date. But it wasn't like we hadn't spent time together.

I didn't know what about the request bothered me. After a moment, though, I decided to chalk it up to shattered nerves—the result of a harrowing evening, followed by an unprovoked mongoose attack.

"God, yes, I do," I said. After all, it was still comparatively early, even after everything that had happened.

"We can take my truck. It's just over here. I'll bring you back to your car later." He gestured out into the parking lot and I followed him to his truck, next to a lamp post under a pool of yellow light. "I need to stop by my house first. Is that okay?"

"Sure. Okay." I ignored the tiny warning bells going off in my head.

Shut up, I told the inner voice. *You're just anxious. It's been a weird night.*

He clicked the key fob and opened the door for me, and I crawled up into the cab, just as I had done on many other occasions.

But for just an instant, as he slammed the door shut, I caught a strange look on his face: oddly intent. Victorious, even.

And definitely not like Scott.

THE DÉCOR in Scott's house was somewhere between *masculine* and *bare*—lots of brown leather furniture, a large-screen television, a simple wood table in the dining area. Scott disappeared around the dividing wall that led into the kitchen.

I should have said no to the invitation. I knew it as soon as "Okay" came out of my mouth.

There was a reason I'd always kept Scott at arm's length. Something about him just didn't work for me.

Maybe because he isn't honor-bound to try to kill you if you get too snaky?

I shushed my snarky internal voice, even as I wondered if maybe it was right—maybe my attraction to Kade was based as much on the danger he represented as anything more stable.

As a trained counselor, I should know better. But if my training and experience had taught me anything, it was that we don't always do what we know is best.

Still, that glimpse of Scott's expression put me enough on edge that when he walked up behind me in his living room and handed me a beer by reaching around me, I almost jumped.

"Interesting pictures." I stepped away from him,

moving along the nearest wall to examine the wildlife photos, all hung at museum-approved eye level.

Most of them were of live animals: cheetahs running across a savannah, monkeys perched in trees, a bright green lizard clinging upside down to a tree, its bright eyes staring at something past the camera.

But several of them were hunting-trophy photos of Scott kneeling over dead animals, rifle in hand, a broad grin splitting his face.

The gleam in his eyes in those photos was disturbingly reminiscent of the expression I had surprised on his face earlier.

I took a sip of the beer to cover my shiver of reaction to the expression. "I didn't know you were a hunter."

Scott moved up beside me to stare at the nearest picture of himself holding the head of a buck up by the antlers. "Reminds me of where I come from."

His smile crooked up only one side of his mouth, and his shrug seemed more rueful than dismissive.

"You come from hunters?" I realized in that moment that in all the conversations we'd had over lunches in the past year, Scott had never once mentioned family.

"You might be surprised."

"That doesn't seem all that odd. We are in Texas, after all." I tried to inject a teasing tone into my voice, but it came out flat.

Scott's response didn't carry any particular inflection. "Yeah." Tilting his head back, he drained the remainder of his beer in one long swallow.

I didn't follow his example, exactly, but I did take another long drink as I continued to peruse the pictures.

Scott leaned against one arm of his brown leather sofa and watched me, his face as expressionless as his voice had been moments ago. The longer he stared, the more uncomfortable I got. I tried to hide my discomfort in another drink.

When I got to the corner of the room and turned to look at the next group of pictures on the adjoining wall, the room spun around me. Reaching out to steady myself against the wall, I realized that my hand was numb. I could barely feel the textured paint under my fingertips.

What the hell was this?

"There it is," Scott said, more emotion coming through his voice than I had heard all night.

I tried to ask, "What's going on?" but I only got as far as "Whuuu" before my legs gave out under me and I crumpled to the floor, my fingers trailing along the wall, doing nothing to stop my fall.

Shift, my mind urged, but my body remained unresponsive.

For the first time ever, I remained human when I wanted to be snake. My thoughts turned sluggish.

The drink. He must have put something in the drink.

But why?

His face appeared in my field of vision, looming over me, then retreating, as my eyes refused to track his motion.

Then he was lifting me, moving me to another room, where he unceremoniously dropped me on the bed. Through the muddled, cottony haze muffling my thoughts, I heard him muttering.

"I can't believe I missed it. Fucking lamia in my *job* and I didn't even see it. How the hell did you hide it?"

He knew what I was? How?

"I have to take you in. I can't just let you go on, living your life." His voice grew louder, more strident. "Stepping in to save those little shapeshifter bitches. How could you?

You know what they are. Abominations. You fucking whore. You ... you *traitor*." The last word came out on a screech, and he reared back. I saw his fist coming toward my face, but could do nothing to avoid it. The crunch when it hit my cheek was audible, and if I could have cringed, I would have —but I barely felt the blow land, as if the pain were coming to me from several miles away.

Traitor?

Oh, God. Scott was involved in the shapeshifter murders, somehow.

I struggled to maintain consciousness, to work through all the implications of what he had said.

Either the punch or whatever he had put in the drink finally overcame my ability to keep my eyes open, though. Darkness edged across my vision. The last thing I saw was Scott, leaning over me, arms outstretched as if to pick me up again.

No, I screamed, but no sound came out.

I CAME to in the dark, lying down on my side, the cold smell of damp limestone clinging to the back of my throat.

Where the hell was I? With one hand, I pushed against the rock beneath me and sat up slowly. Blinking hard, I peered into the darkness surrounding me.

Nothing. I might as well have my eyes closed. But the space around me felt big, somehow.

The blow to my face—or maybe the drugs, or maybe the combination of the two—left me feeling groggy and disoriented.

Why had he conked me over the head and dragged me into a cave? What the hell was Scott into?

Other than being a crazy murderer.

Though on second thought, he might not need any more reason than that.

I had dismissed Moreland's comment about not calling Scott. I shouldn't have.

And why, oh why hadn't I told Kade where I was headed?

Because he hadn't been in the most receptive mood ever.

And because I hadn't been certain that *he* wasn't likely to hit me over the head and drag me off somewhere— though in Kade's case, he probably would have claimed it was for my own good.

For that matter, it might have been the better option, given my current situation.

Which was what, exactly?

I flicked my tongue out and tasted the air. Water. A lot of stone. Cold air moving in a steady breeze from my left. The faint flavor of smoke carried on that wind.

Cautiously, I stretched my hands above me as far as they would go, then out to the sides, in front, and behind me. The idea of stumbling around in the dark didn't appeal to me, and probably wouldn't be all that productive, anyway—not unless I had some way to track where I was going, and where I had been. Unlikely in this stygian blackness.

At some point, Scott had taken off my shoes, leaving only stockings. Between that and my thin work blouse, the cool air of the cave was beginning to get to me. Chill bumps raced up and down my arms and I ran my hands up and down, trying to generate warmth.

I didn't know if I could reasonably shift in here, or if the chill would immobilize me.

And if Scott knew what I was? That might very well be why he'd brought me here.

A pebble lodged under me gave me an idea, though. I scrabbled around on the floor and gathered it and several others. One by one, I tossed them out as hard as I could in what I was pretty sure were different directions. Two of them hit the floor and kept rolling, eventually clattering to a stop on their own. The others hit obstacles and bounced back toward me.

I considered shifting, exploring the cavern in my animal form, but the chill in the air suggested that might be a bad idea. I wanted to be able to move quickly, and the cold was making me feel sluggish in my human form. My serpent shape was likely to go into hibernation mode.

But I could still use those animal senses to some degree. And that cold draft had to be coming from somewhere. Wind didn't just create itself in a cave. That air led to an exit of some kind.

I closed my eyes and let myself follow the air, flicking my tongue out every few seconds. Initially, I held my hands out in front of me to avoid bumping into any cavern walls. After a few moments, though, I dropped my arms to my sides and paused long enough to concentrate on the partial shift Kade had been trying to teach me. I concentrated on my mouth, on feeling my tongue split, the Jacobson's organ grow where my soft palate had been. Apparently the sheer terror I'd been tamping down since I woke had a beneficial effect on my partial-shift ability—though I also felt my fangs descending and my jaw changing shape before I stopped the transformation. I suspected that if I could see, I would discover that my vision had altered, along with my eyes.

Whatever. I still had my mammalian ability to regulate

my own body temperature, important given the fact that I was walking straight into the chilly airstream.

I don't know how long I walked, trusting my serpent senses to warn me before I bumped into cave walls, before I sensed a change in the air current I was following. That hint of smoke had grown stronger, and it was coming in from a different direction, a separate strand of wind, weaving itself in and around the colder, cleaner breeze I had been following. This one smelled of campfires—wood and dirt, with an under layer of humanity.

Soon afterwards, the floor beneath my feet began to tilt upwards. Up and out, I hoped. The wood smoke scent grew ever stronger, until I reached a place where the two scents, the cold air and the smoke, came from different directions.

Finally, I opened my eyes.

I was unsurprised to realize that my eyes had, indeed, shifted, and that what I could see in the dim light flickering in from an unknown source was all in black and white.

But I was extraordinarily surprised to see, dancing in front of my eyes, the flickering, twinkling lights of the Earth magic Kade had shown me. I hadn't realized it was there, but when I concentrated, I could feel it thrumming beneath my feet and through the walls surrounding me.

Blinking away the sparkles, I took stock. I stood at a T-junction in the path, the cold air blowing in from one direction, the wood smoke from the other.

The smart thing to do would be to follow the breeze to the closest exit, get the hell out of here, and find a way to get home. I didn't know what Scott had in mind, but knocking a girl out and stuffing her into a cave rarely led to a pleasant outcome.

Not even on the third date.

But every instinct I had told me that whatever he had planned was wrapped up in whatever was going on in the cavern to my right, the one with the smoke and the people. The one that I definitely should avoid.

So I turned right.

Every so often, I passed fissures in the rock. Streams of air blew out from some of them, but none of them seemed to lead to obvious passages. And none of the breezes were as strong as the one I followed, so I stayed in the main tunnel, trying to remain quiet as my shoes scuffed along the pebble-strewn floor.

I kept my eyes open the whole time now and checked the air more often, hoping for some warning if someone moved toward me.

No one did.

Instead, I followed the smell of smoke up a well-worn path until the scent was joined by flickering firelight. At that point, I slowed and listened, but my partial shift had apparently included my ears. I heard some sort of movement and the echoing of a high-pitched voice, but not well enough to make out words.

A few yards further, the tunnel curved away to the left. I peeked around the corner. The tunnel widened into an entrance to another cavern. Firelight reflected from the walls, and as I watched, sparks shot up into the air from the fire somewhere inside.

I ducked back, flattening myself against the wall.

Not for the first time, I cursed my limited serpent hearing. My sense of smell almost made up for it, but not entirely. Again, I tasted the air. The tang of humanity that had been merely an undertone to the smoke earlier now threatened to overwhelm it, a stench of fear and anger, of unwashed bodies, at least ten of them. And mingling with it all, the smell of ... Scott.

What the hell was going on?

Moving slowly enough to avoid making any noise, I

pulled on the Earth magic, hard, drawing it into myself as much as possible, pulling it around me. I didn't know if it could conceal me, but I wanted to try.

This time, I concentrated on my serpentine skills. Not the physical form, but my ability to slide silently along the floor, to move unnoticed, to blend with the world around me. I was an unseen predator, camouflaged by my very skin.

My movements smoothed out even as the sparkles popped in front of my eyes, shimmering and dancing. Gliding gracefully, I skimmed across the ground and up to the cavern entrance.

The room was large and round, with stalactites hanging down from the ceiling. Blackened rocks surrounded the fire pit in the middle of the room, and most of the smoke rose up through a small chimney-hole in the ceiling, leaving soot smudges in a circle around it. The flickering firelight didn't reach the walls, though, leaving most of the room without illumination. Boxes lined the edges of the room, covered with dark tarps.

I saw Scott first, leaning on what initially looked like a box. Movement inside it caught my attention, though, and I realized it wasn't solid. It had thick metal bars. And inside the cage was what looked like a human woman. Scott was leaning over her, talking to her as she cowered as far away from him as possible, her arms wrapped around her naked body.

The flavor of lust roiled off Scott, and the more she cringed, the stronger the taste became.

Then I realized that the scent of fear came from several points in the room.

All of the boxes were cages, and they all contained women. And every one of them was terrified of the sound of Scott's voice.

I might have moved in at that point, except that another figure slithered out of a recess in the very back of the room.

This one was female, too, but was only human from the waist up.

The rest of her was all snake.

There was another lamia in the world.

And Scott knew her.

THE LAMIA WAS OLDER, probably earlier fifties, assuming we aged like humans.

Something else to ask Kade, if I lived through this.

Her snake half was huge, big enough to support the torso of an average-size woman, and the pattern of scales blended in nicely with the floor and walls of the cavern, very much as I had imagined myself moments earlier.

She didn't wear a shirt, and her breasts swung pendulously as she moved into the room. Her hair looked like it hadn't seen a brush in far too long. I suspected it would be blonde if it were washed and brushed—and if I had my human color vision. But it hung in long hanks, almost like dreadlocks.

As she moved toward Scott, she said something I couldn't make out, then flicked her own tongue out, testing the air around her.

And then she froze in place, like a snake catching the scent of prey—which I guess she was.

Only I suspected that for the first time in a long time, I was the prey.

I pulled the sparkling Earth magic closer around me, tightening it like a cloak, even as I wished I could better hear what the lamia woman was saying. As if in response to my wish, my ears shifted back to their human form, and I heard a sibilant female voice. "There is someone here, Scott."

My erstwhile date stood up straight and glanced around. "You're imagining things, mother. Don't be paranoid."

Mother? Oh, hell. I was in deep trouble.

CHAPTER
TWENTY-ONE

I didn't know if the Earth magic was really keeping them from noticing me, but just in case, I concentrated on pulling it even tighter around me.

"You should not have brought her," the lamia said in apparent continuation of an earlier discussion.

About the girl in the cage, or about me?

"She's different, Mother," Scott said. "She's a shifter."

Scott's mother was a lamia. Holy shit.

"We've tried other shifters before. It didn't work." The mother slithered closer to him, shaking her head. Beads knotted into the dreadlocks clicked as she moved.

Her son didn't look at her as he picked up a canvas tarp from the floor and draped it over the cage. From inside came a whimper, whether from terror or relief, I couldn't tell. Neither Scott nor his mother paid any attention to the noise, but Scott carefully smoothed out the covering as he spoke. "She's a snake shifter, Mother."

The lamia's attention had turned elsewhere, but at his words, she whipped around toward him, beaded dreads flying out around her head. Her lower body undulated wildly as she advanced on her son, the end of her tail twitching wildly, like some crazed Medusa.

"You found another lamia?" she hissed, leaning over Scott. He cringed away from her in much the same way that the girl in the cage had cringed from him. "And you brought her here? Without telling me?"

Scott covered his head with both arms as his mother moved closer, raising up on the tip of her tail and looming above him. Her eyes narrowed and her nostrils flared as she leaned over him. Even as far away as I was, I could taste the bitter flavor of fear as it roiled off him.

How awful was this woman, if her own son feared her that much?

Almost certainly as bad as the rest of the lamias, whose extermination had been accepted among other shapeshifters. Maybe worse. After all, her son—and maybe she?—had at least a dozen women in cages in a cave.

And I was dating the son-of-a-bitch.

Was being the key word.

As Daniel Moreland so often said, some sons-a-bitches needed killing.

I was pretty sure Scott was one of them.

"Take me to her," the lamia said.

Crap. I needed to retreat.

There was no way I was going to let Scott and his mother find me again. For as long as they didn't know where I was, I had the upper hand. I couldn't stay here, though, even with the sparkling magic pulled around me.

As silently as possible, I stepped backwards, stopping briefly when a pebble rolled under my mostly bare foot. When the lamia and her son didn't look up or raise an alarm, I moved more quickly, feeling my way back down the hallway.

Around the curve in the tunnel and halfway back to the

T-junction, I heard them behind me. Rather than risk being caught, I ducked into one of the fissures in the wall, wedging myself in as tightly as possible. There was no air flowing through this one, no possible back exit. If they found me now, I was trapped. My heart pounded in my chest and I held my breath, concentrating as hard as I could on pulling the Earth magic into myself.

The sparkles in my vision grew so intense that I closed my eyes entirely, relying upon other senses to tell when the two passed my cramped hiding spot. I could smell them coming, Scott tasting of flop-sweat and terror, his mother of ... something colder. Darker. Something I had never scented before.

Something that called to a part of me I had worked hard to suppress.

I shivered, despite my determination to remain perfectly still.

Scott was talking as they moved past me. "But the genetics are right. She's the best shot we'll ever have." His wheedling tone was nothing like anything I had heard from him before.

"Perhaps. But we need to know who she is, first. Where did she come from?" The rustling of the lamia's scales passing by called to me, touching a deep yearning in my heart that I hadn't even known was there. The same feeling that drew me to coil up with Suzy in my father's herpetarium.

The call of like to like.

I shoved the desire away, tamping it down with a ferocity that came of the knowledge that as much as I longed to know more of my own species, this woman was not the way to do it.

This was a woman who seemed to be encouraging her son in some sort of genetic experiment.

She and I were not of a kind, even if we shared a species —or merely a phylum.

Ultimately, that was what drew me back to the cavern with the cages.

I couldn't simply leave all those women locked up, even if I planned to go for help. Whatever it was that Scott and his mother were doing, I didn't believe it could possibly be good.

So when I stepped out of the crevasse after they had made another turn in the tunnel, instead of following the stream of cold air to what I presumed was the exit, I made my way back to the room with the firelight and tarpaulin-covered cages.

Having grown used to the sensory input my partial shift gave me, I almost forgot to transform back into my human shape before I ripped the cover off the first cage. At the last minute, though, I was hit with the image of a woman's screams drawing the lamia and Scott back before I could get any of the women out.

As it turned out, though, I was the one who almost screamed when I removed the canvas from the cage nearest the door.

Like the other woman I had seen, the girl in this cage was naked and cowering at the back of her enclosure. She was young, too, no more than sixteen or seventeen.

And she was heavily pregnant.

THE PREGNANT WOMAN in the cage didn't scream, but she did whimper and cringe into the back corner. When she finally looked up and realized that I wasn't Scott or his mother, she burst into motion, scrabbling across the bottom of the enclosure toward me.

"Get me out of here." Her voice was hoarse, as if she had screamed her throat raw.

Maybe she had.

"I don't know how," I whispered, fumbling with the heavy padlock that kept the door closed. "Do you know where the key is?"

She shook her head mutely, tears gathering in the corners of her eyes.

A knot formed in my stomach as I glanced around at the room full of crates, then back to the pregnant woman. "How many of you are there?"

With a shrug, she used the back of her hand to dash the moisture from her eyes. "It varies. Depends on how the ..." Pausing, she glanced down at her swollen belly and sneered. "How the breeding program is going."

Bile rose in my throat. I had to ask, though I already knew the answer. "What's the goal of all this?"

"Monsters." Her ravaged voice dropped even lower. "He wants to make more monsters, just like his mother."

I had let that psycho kiss me.

Dear God.

"Who's there?" an anxious voice wavered from one of the other covered boxes. "Please help us."

Part of me wanted to uncover every one of the miniature cells lining the room, look every single woman in the eye, let her know that help was coming.

But I didn't have time.

"I'm going to get you out of here," I said, raising my voice a little. "I'm going to get us all out of here. Please just hold on a little longer."

The woman in the uncovered cage stared at me blankly, disbelieving.

"What's your name?" I asked, squatting down next to the cage until we were eye-to-eye.

"Carrie," she said.

"I'm coming back for all of you. But for that to happen, I'm going to have to put the canvas back over this box. Can you handle that, Carrie?" When she didn't answer immediately, I wrapped my fingers around the bars, covering her own hand. "I'm going for help. I will be back."

Carrie's mouth tightened, but she nodded.

She held my gaze with her own as I dropped the covering back over her.

Breeding program.

Kill off the other shapeshifters' children. Make his own.

It really was a diabolical plan.

Horrific.

I shuddered as I made a quick circuit of the room, hoping that Scott might have left the keys somewhere visible, even though I was absolutely sure they were on that enormous, jangling keychain of his.

If only I'd grabbed it when I had the chance.

I was going to have to get out of the cavern system entirely, go for help. And I needed to do it before the lamia and her son returned.

"I'll be back," I said again, just loudly enough for everyone to hear me.

The sound of quiet sobbing followed me as I slid out of the room and down the passageway.

When I reached the crack in the wall I had hidden in earlier, I stopped to listen. Hearing nothing, I once again shifted my mouth and jaw enough to taste the air. The scent of Scott and his mother flavored the air, but the tang of their passing wasn't new. They were still down in the cavern, presumably searching for me.

At the T-junction, the draft from outside grew stronger, blowing away any other smells. If I went that way, my own scent would be blown back toward the cavern.

Scott's mother would be able to tell which way I had gone.

Still, there was no way in hell I was sticking around. The floor of the tunnel tilted up toward the surface, and with the loss of information from the cavern scents, I found myself running, ignoring the way the occasional pebbles along the ground cut into the soles of my feet.

By the time I reached the cavern entrance, I was panting and running so hard that I almost ran outside without looking where I was going. At the last minute, though, I skidded to a halt, grabbing one side of the cave entrance and hanging on tightly.

I found myself high on a cliff wall, dangling above the river below—the Paluxy, I assumed, though for all I knew, I could have been out for hours and hours and they could've carried me to a river even farther away from Fort Worth.

But dawn was still far from beginning to cast a pink glow on the horizon, and nothing about my situation suggested I had been out for more than a short while. I wasn't hungry or thirsty. I hadn't even needed to pee when I woke up.

That also meant that no one had missed me yet.

I wasn't on call this weekend, so no one would expect me at work until Monday.

And after our last discussion, Kade wouldn't be expecting me to come back at all.

I was on my own, and all of those poor women back there in those cages were counting on me to save them.

Taking a deep breath, I leaned out to assess the cliff face. It wasn't really perfectly vertical. It only seemed that way from my human perspective. There were small outcroppings of rock. Small plants had taken root in the cliff and grew straight out into the air.

Nothing strong enough to hold a human's weight.

But a snake could make it.

Not a large snake—nothing the size of Suzy, or even my usual shifting form.

But something small and quick could make it down to the river. I glanced upwards, too, but didn't know where the cliff-top came out. At least by following the riverbed, I should eventually come to some form of civilization.

I only hoped it would be soon enough for the women inside.

Taking a deep breath, I focused on Kade's instructions, imagining the shift I wanted to make, always holding my goal in my mind.

Again, I pulled on the Earth magic, surrounding myself with it, pulling it into me, through me. Color leached from the world as my eyes changed first.

Small.

Fast.

To the river, then home.

This time, the shift ripped through me, a burning pain that cauterized my limbs to me, ripping away mass and replacing it with pure, blazing magic, white-hot and searing.

If I could have screamed, I would have.

Instead, when I came out of the change, I was already moving.

Down toward the river. Dropping from a clump of grass to a stone ledge only an inch wide, sliding over to catch the next plant.

Always down.

I lost track of time.

The sun came up fully, warming me even as the last of my mammalian heat faded.

At some point, I felt the vibrations of shouts, almost understood the words. But they were human words, human needs. They had nothing to do with me. I was small and quick, slipping past other creatures unnoticed, stopping only long enough to scent the air, find the next way down toward the water.

Once, the scent of rodent in the air drew me, and I almost stopped to hunt. But some compulsion drove me on.

Down.

To the water.

When I finally reached the river, I paused, confused.

I wasn't thirsty. Why had I come to the water?

What now?

Smoke drifted through the air.

Danger.

But contained. Not a grass fire.

Human.

The word campfire flashed through my mind.

Campfire.

Shift.

I was far enough away now.

Be the change I need to be.

Shift, that inner voice commanded. A voice that was mine, but not mine.

I am serpent.

No, another part of me remembered.

Shift. Human.

The moonlight glinted on the water.

No. Not human. Not yet.

Concentrating, I pushed my way into a water-form.

Water moccasin. Sleek and black and able to cross the river easily.

I slipped into the water and continued toward the campgrounds.

～

Kade.

His name echoed through my mind, long after I had forgotten anything else about why I was traveling, or why. I merely whipped my body from side to side, moving as quickly as I could through the landscape.

When I finally came upon a human campsite, I paused, certain that it was important in some way. Flicking my tongue out, I pulled in the warm night air, redolent of campfire smoke and the taste of human sweat and sleep. Safe enough to explore.

Why did I need to stop here?

I raised up as high as I could, weaving back and forth, testing the air.

There. Something sun-warmed and slightly damp with river-water, permeated with humanity.

Then I saw it: a rope line stretched between two trees with several bathing suits and t-shirts, left out to dry after a dip in the river.

The human part of my mind struggled to form thoughts, trapped as it was deep inside my serpentine brain.

Kade.

These would help me reach Kade.

But first I had to find a place to shift.

Retreating into the scrubby trees a few yards away, I pulled on the Earth magic again, working to draw mass back to myself. The magic was weaker here than it had been even at the cave. In my serpent form, my concentration wavered, making it harder to draw on that power. My entire body convulsed with the effort, and then, as if something inside me snapped, the sparkling light coalesced around me, pouring into the shift. When the glare faded from my eyes, I lay curled in a tight ball, whimpering.

Get up, Lindi.

You have to get help to save those women.

Even my growing sense of desperation couldn't force my aching muscles to move more quickly. Nonetheless, I pulled myself up to standing and staggered toward the clothesline.

Several pairs of men's swim trunks hung from the rope. I tugged down the smallest pair and stepped into them, tying the drawstring tight around my waist.

Pulling a stolen t-shirt over my head, I considered my next move. My head pounded. Too many shifts in too short a time combined with a lack of food or drink, and who knew what drugs Scott had slipped me, making me dizzy and sick.

I could wake these campers, beg them for help, see if any of them had a cell phone. Or I could keep moving, try to find a better way out of here.

Wherever *here* was.

I didn't see any cars. These people must have back-packed in from somewhere else. I vaguely recalled that the Dinosaur Valley park had camping areas that were inaccessible by car.

God. I couldn't think straight.

I didn't even have any shoes.

Perhaps that, at least, could be remedied. I scanned the small clearing, looking for anything useful.

Spying a pair of men's flip-flops, I slid my toes into them. A plastic cooler sitting right outside the tent looked promising, too. These guys hadn't had to hike too far in if one of them had lugged that.

As quietly as I could, I unlatched the lid and swung it open. Inside were several cans of beer, a few water bottles, and a package of lunch meat.

I grabbed the meat and some of the water.

I couldn't be that far from the parking lot. And from there, it was only a short walk to the ranger's hut.

Involving normal humans was a bad idea. Given his treatment of shifter children and human women, I suspected that Scott wouldn't hesitate to murder the men who were camping here, out for a guys' weekend, from the looks of it.

I would never be able to forgive myself if I got them killed.

Retreating again to the cover of the foliage surrounding the campsite, I downed one bottle of water before skirting the site and moving back down along the river. Walking as quickly as I could while eating, I ate the entire package of lunch meat. I wasn't used to shifting this much so quickly, and that last change felt like something had torn inside me. I could only hope that my usually accelerated healing worked for magical injuries, too.

The food and water helped some. At least my head wasn't throbbing any longer. I felt like I was thinking more clearly. But it was taking longer than usual to regain all my human faculties, maybe as a side-effect of choosing an animal shape so different from my usual one. I was far from the campers' site when it finally occurred to me that there had probably been a trail directly from the campers' clearing back to the parking lot, and from the lot to the ranger.

I wondered how much of my determination to stick to the cover that ran right next to the river came from my animal side. It felt safer, even as my human mind high-lighted the logic of searching for a trail.

As comforting as I found it to follow the river, it was time to change my strategy, I decided. But then, as I swung around a bend in the river, I realized that I wouldn't have to. Just in front of me was the swimming hole with the fossilized dinosaur print on its edge.

I knew exactly where I was and where to go from here.

Now I just needed to find Kade.

I considered what I knew as I waded through the shallow water.

Scott was fully human—I was certain of it. I might not have recognized shifter scents before, but the last few weeks had driven home the differences between how humans and shifters smelled.

But that didn't mean he didn't carry a lamia gene.

I tried to remember Kade's mini-lecture about shapeshifter genetics. If Scott really was trying to breed with humans to create new lamias, it meant he would need a human woman who had lamia genes.

Given what little I knew about lamia culture, I doubted there were very many cross-breeds out there.

How many women had Scott raped in this crazed plan? How many had he killed?

I had to get help.

TWENTY-TWO

I'm pretty sure the park ranger manning the entry booth thought I was crazy when I came stumbling up to her window in my stolen, too-big clothes and shoes, clutching a wad of bologna in one hand and an empty water bottle in the other.

"Phone," I gasped. "I need to use your phone. It's an emergency."

"Can I help you with something, sweetie?" she asked, her thin lips twisted in worry. "Is there a problem with your campsite?"

In the several hours it had taken me to get here, it had never occurred to me that I would have to come up with a story to cover what was really going on.

I couldn't tell this muscular woman in her khaki shorts and green shirt that a snake woman and her rapist son were trying to breed a new race of lamias.

She would think I was nuts.

I had to reach Kade.

What would she believe?

"My boyfriend and I had a fight last night and he left.

My phone, my clothes, everything was in the car. Please, I just need to reach a friend to come pick me up." There. That should do it.

With a nod, she opened the door to the booth and ushered me in, pointing to a stool in one corner. "Have a seat. The phone is right there on the counter."

～

"When they find me gone, they're going to realize something has happened," I said into the phone receiver. The ranger had draped a blanket around me and given me the nominal privacy of the booth as she stepped out to make a few phone calls on her cell.

"If you've been gone as long as you think, they probably already have." Kade's voice echoed across the miles. He was already headed toward me—had been in his truck searching for hours and wasn't very far away at all.

I shrugged, though he couldn't see it. "My sense of time is completely screwed up. It feels like hours, but this is the first time I've . . ." My voice trailed off. "Well, that I've been that small."

"That can definitely trash your senses. It's not something many of us do very often." With a rumble, his pickup came around the gravel in the drive. "There you are," he said into the phone, waving at me through the windshield as he swiped off the receiver.

Kade had food for me in the Jeep, and he was silent while I devoured five burgers, one right after the other. When I finally leaned back against the headrest of the passenger seat and blew out a breath, he said quietly, "You're going to have to go back, you know."

We had pulled over into a spot in the parking lot, and

the park ranger was studiously—and kindly, too, I thought—ignoring us.

I had thought the same thing, but I wasn't sure how I was going to get back to the caves, back in to both rescue the women there and take out Scott and his mother.

"They're bound to have noticed I'm gone by now," I said. "They might have left to search for me."

"With any luck," Kade agreed.

"So do we wait for the rest of the Council?" Opening a third bottle of water, I downed it. The additional food and water continued to help, but deep inside there was still something not right.

"I don't think we can wait." Kade gathered the wrappers from my burgers and stuffed them into their paper sack. "We need to get those women out of there."

"There's more," I said. "I think they're also the ones who have been killing shifter children." Kade didn't respond, but the sharp scent of anger spiked around him. "Scott showed up at the motel earlier. But I didn't call him, and neither did Moreland. And he was there before anyone else."

Kade nodded. "So you think he was meeting his mother there?"

"Yes. Did any of the girls talk before you left the hospital?"

"No. I left not more than fifteen minutes after you did." He paused, glancing at me out of the corner of one swirling, golden eye. "I wanted to find you, to apologize. I had no right to grab you like that."

Now the flavor that rolled through the cab of the Jeep carried a hint of anxiety with it as well. "I'm sorry, Lindi."

Part of me wanted to stay angry with him, but I didn't have the energy. Besides, when I'd been in danger, the thought of him was what had kept me going, what had allowed me to hang on to the human part of myself. "It's okay. We can work out anything about us later. For now, we need to do what we can to save the women Scott has locked in those cages."

IN THE END, we decided to take the easiest way in.

For us, that meant hiking in as human, then shifting if we needed to fight Scott and his mother.

Kade talked to the ranger. I'm not sure what he told her —probably something about making sure we had all of my belongings—but in any case, she gave him a permit and let us drive in and park the Jeep in one of the lots that fronted the hiking trails.

And then we began tracing my steps, backtracking along my trail to find the cavern that held half a dozen women who, as far as I knew, may never have even been reported missing.

Again, we passed the campsite where I had stolen the clothes, and I returned the t-shirt in favor of an extra one that had been in the back of Kade's Jeep.

When we crossed the river, Kade paused and sniffed the air, then scanned the ground around us. "Did you stick to the river most of the way?" he asked.

"I think so." I scanned the ground and tasted the air. "I don't remember all of it. But any time I started to veer off the trail, I reminded myself to stick to the river, right up to the point that I found the campground and shifted."

"If the caves they're using are the ones I think they must be, then we'll make better time if we go cross-country here."

"And if they're not?"

Kade's brow furrowed as he peered into the dark

surrounding us. "If they're not the caves I know of, then we'll have to come back and start over."

I flicked my tongue out to test the air. "It's getting close to morning now. I'm worried that they might do something to the women before we can get to them, especially if we have to backtrack."

"I don't think that's very likely. In any case, though, we'll be following the river until we get to a pass through the cliffs." I followed behind him, watching the sky above for signs of the approaching dawn.

IN MY SMALLER SERPENT FORM, it felt like it had taken hours to get back to the state park's main campsites. I didn't know how much of that was due to the strange change that subjective time took on while I was in that undersized body, but it took us less than two hours to make it back to the base of the caves in our human shapes.

By the time we got there, the sky was beginning to lighten, to turn gray in the early morning.

As soon as we could see the cavern openings, we ducked down into the scrubby foliage nearby and watched for any activity.

Nothing moved. Either our presence or the lamia in the cavern had silenced the wildlife around us. The morning remained eerily silent.

Finally, Kade motioned me further away from the cliff faces. After we had retreated a sufficient distance, he put his mouth up against my ear and whispered. "I think we should come at the entrance from different directions, double our chances of getting in and setting those women free."

I nodded, cupping my hands around my mouth and

hissing a response. "When should the Council members be here?"

"I left messages for Eduardo and Janice. Neither answered, so I'm not sure when they'll head out." He pulled his phone out of the pocket of his jeans and waved it in the air a little, checking for a signal. "Nope. We may be in this alone."

Okay. I could do this.

I nodded. "So how do we approach them?"

Kade pulled a twig off the ground, then knelt, sketching out a map in the dirt in front of us. "If I'm remembering correctly, there's a path that takes you up the cliff about here." He pointed to a spot east of us. "That's the route that they're most likely to take if they're coming down, but it's also the easiest to navigate. You take that one, but be prepared to hide, and to shift, if necessary."

He checked to make sure I was following his explanation. "This direction"—he pointed at the west side of the hastily sketched map—"will take me up to the top of the cliff. It's a tougher climb and there are fewer places to hide, but it's a trade-off, because I think they're less likely to go this way, unless they have a car parked somewhere on one of the roads above. If you want this route, you can have it."

"Is our goal to stop them, or to get to the women?" I crouched down next to him.

"Get to the women first. Stop them if we can." He watched me with those swirling eyes and waited for my response.

"Then I'll take the lower trail."

"If they come up on you, do your best to hide." As he stood, Kade wiped out the dirt map. "Other than that, just work on getting the women free. But watch this." Twirling one hand above the ground, he stared hard at the dirt.

Within seconds, bright glints of light shimmered around his arm.

"The Earth magic," I said.

"Use it if you need to. Don't hesitate to shift if necessary, and take the most powerful form you can."

"I will." I turned to head back toward the cliff, but before I could take a step away, Kade spun me into his arms and crushed his lips to mine, hard and demanding at first, then softer. The taste of him changed, swirling into something that tasted like his eyes looked when he watched me. Something as soft as it was passionate.

When he pulled away, he whispered, "I'm sorry I yelled at you at the hospital. I panicked."

"I think coming out to save me from the crazed lamia and her psycho son more than covers that." I grinned, unable to hold back the expression, even in the midst of this insane rescue mission.

"If you get to the women first, get them up to the top of the cliff and head north to the road," Kade said. "We'll meet there, no matter what." He paused. "But don't wait for me. You flag down the first passing car you see and get them to the nearest hospital. Then call Kindred. Someone there will help you."

I nodded, a knot forming in my stomach. There were so many ways this plan, thrown together as it was, could go awry.

Kade pulled me in for a last, hard kiss. "Be careful," he whispered.

And then we split up, headed for opposite sides of the cliff face.

∾

I HAD BEEN MAKING my way up the path for less than five minutes when I heard someone skittering down the trail above me, around a slight bend.

"If she went down this way, she's long gone, Mother," I heard Scott say.

They were both here, then.

Slowly, I stepped backwards down the trail to the last indentation I had seen in the wall, right at the junction of a tiny clearing that formed a wide spot in the trail.

Pulling back, I slipped into a crevasse in the rocks, drawing my arms and legs in after me. It wasn't a deep fissure—there was no way I could keep them from seeing me.

I would have to fight.

But honestly, I had known it would come to this from the moment I had seen the other lamia. Something primitive deep within me had told me from the very beginning that she and I would clash. That one of us would end the other.

I closed my eyes and pushed into a shift. The world around me grayed out. At the same time, I tugged at the power I could feel thrumming beneath my feet. The diamante sparkles flashed into being around me, and for the first time ever, terror didn't overcome me in the moment that I slipped from human to serpent.

I wasn't losing my arms and legs, my mobility, my humanity.

I was taking on my power-form.

And I flowed into it.

Kade's advice echoed through my mind. *Be the change you need.*

Not just my need, though. Also Emma's need, and Kirstie's, and the other girls from the motel, whose names I didn't know yet. All the women in the cave above me I hoped to rescue. And all those shifter-children whose lives I had not been able to save.

The glittering, shifting mist swirled around me faster and faster, and I followed it out of the crack in the rocks, stretching up higher and higher to wrap myself around it, in it, letting it flow through me, closing my eyelids one last time as they became transparent and froze into the brille, a scaly eyelid protecting my eyes.

When I slid out from behind the rocks into the clearing, Scott gasped.

Rising as high as I could into striking position, I towered above him.

The shape I need.

At least twenty-five feet long, some deep, clinical part of my brain noted. And patterned much like Suzy—but where she was yellow, my scales rippled with a blue-white shine that echoed the magical light of the earth-power I had drawn upon.

I shouldn't have been able to see the color.

But I did.

With a hiss, I drew in the tastes of the world around me.

Fear flowed from Scott into my mouth, sliding down my throat like honey, slow and sweet and delicious.

But underlying the fear were the other flavors, the lust he had inflicted on the women he had attempted to breed, the joy he had taken in capturing the offspring of other shifters, the rush of power he felt as he killed them.

The scent of horror stained him, rotting the sweetness of his fear.

And threading through it all, permeating every other smell, was his connection to his mother. I don't know how I had missed it before—though perhaps its very pervasiveness had fooled me into thinking it was simply part of his own scent, rather than something foreign that had wormed its way into his signature smell.

In any case, I now recognized it as maternal and serpentine. As something that shouldn't be there, a cancerous rot at the very core of his identity.

With a hiss, I reared back, preparing to strike. Scott threw himself backwards, falling to the ground and scrabbling away from me, one hand up to ward me off as the other clawed the dirt behind him, either to find a weapon or to pull himself toward safety.

His words vibrated through the ground and air, though as I sank deeper and deeper into this form, it took me longer than usual to parse out their meaning. "Please don't. Don't hurt me. Lindi, no." His pleading made me angrier than ever, certain as I was that at least some of his victims —only children—must have begged for their lives, as well.

The women he had raped had probably implored him to stop, too.

He wasn't going to get any more mercy than he had given.

But as I drew back, I felt a wave of heat flow across my face, alerting me to another presence behind me.

Even as I whipped around to assess the new threat, that same scientific part of my mind noted that in this shift, I had apparently taken on the characteristics of more than one species of snake. Suzy, a constrictor, wouldn't have been able to sense body heat the way I had. Pit vipers did that.

Be the change you need.

Apparently I had.

I took in the scent of the new arrival at the same moment that I saw her.

Scott's mother, in her hybrid shape—top half human, bottom half snake.

Using the back quarter of my body, I coiled around Scott and held him in place, tightening my grip as he tried to pull away.

Constrictor.

Flicking my tongue out, I weaved back and forth, waiting for the right moment to strike, my fangs retracted.

Viper.

"Mama, help," Scott gasped. When she didn't respond, he tried again. "Mother. *Tanith.*"

Her name.

It seemed fitting that I know her name before I ended her life.

I had just enough time to realize that her traditional lamia form was really crappy for fighting when Tanith began to morph, her face elongating and the crown of her head flattening into the triangular skull of a viper.

None of the Earth magic sparkled around her, though.

Could she possibly be limited to only one shape?

No time to consider the options now.

I knew from practice on my family's ranch that in my usual serpent shape, I could strike about two-thirds of my body length. I had never struck another person, though. And this person was the only other weresnake I had ever met.

I had no choice.

While I still towered over her, I struck.

Tanith was fast enough, and practiced enough, to whip mostly out of range, but I managed to graze the side of her neck with one fang.

With the very last of her human speech, she snarled, "Bitch." The last of the word faded out on a hiss, and she pulled the bottom half of her body around so she could rear up higher, trying to match my height, her mouth wide open, jaws unhinged and ready to clamp down on me.

She wasn't as long—or as big—as I was, though, and her serpent form incorporated only one breed of snake. The fact that she had gone for the viper form could play out in my favor, as I was, presumably, as immune to her venom as I had been to my fathers' vipers. She would have to try to injure my face and head enough to kill me—because, it suddenly occurred to me, there was no other possible outcome. One of us was going to die today.

I needed to do something with Scott, though. I couldn't continue to hold him still and fight his mother at the same time.

I could kill him, squeeze the breath and life out of him, but the Council wanted him alive for questioning.

Only one idea occurred to me. Tightening my tail around him, I lifted him up several feet and slammed him back down to the ground. His mother hissed at his scream, slithering to one side as she looked for an opportunity to strike.

I matched her move, weaving back and forth to meet her, then pulling around so all she could see was the portion of my body below my neck, offering no effective purchase for her to strike.

Again, I lifted Scott, this time looping another coil of my constrictor body around him to change the angle of my hold so his legs dangled as far above the ground as I could manage while still sliding out of the other lamia's attack zone.

This time when I smashed him down to the ground, I felt the crack of leg bones breaking, even through the reverberation of his shriek.

Scott wouldn't be walking anywhere soon.

The sound of his whimpers sent his mother into a frenzy, striking toward me in short jabs, all easily evaded, until a white-hot burst of fire exploded in my body, ripping down toward my tail. I jerked away from the lamia long enough to discover that Scott had jabbed a Bowie knife into me, slicing a trail of pain through my lower back.

All it took was that instant of inattention for Tanith to sink her fangs into the back of my head.

Stunned, I pulled away, but the lamia twirled around and around, using her body to tighten her grip on me, even as Scott dragged himself closer again and drove his knife through my tail, pinning it to the dirt below.

The human part of my mind froze, overcome by sheer animal instinct. Ignoring the pain, I ripped my tail up, flinging the knife away, and began whipping back and forth, fighting to escape Tanith even as she struggled to maintain her hold.

My frantic motions slammed Scott against the rock face of the cliff, and I lost track of him.

Then, through the coils wrapped around my eyes, I caught a glimpse of a diamond sparkle dropping through the air. Surprised into stillness, I let it touch down on my damaged tail section, where it counteracted the painful burn with a soft warmth.

A healing heat.

Focus, Lindi.

As Tanith clenched her jaw tighter and continued to slide her body around mine to hold my own mouth shut, I forced myself to remain motionless and concentrated on drawing the power surrounding me into myself.

Be the change you need to be.

The muscles of my body knitted together, the scales sliding over them, the wound closing.

Then I began to grow, pulling more and more of the Earth power into my body. Tanith's jaws creaked and the space between her coils expanded. Light flowed into the space, bringing more and more of the glittering sparkles in contact with my scales. They flew in flurries into my eyes, piling up and crusting over them until I saw nothing but silver shine.

The feel of Tanith's hold on me melted away until it was little more than a nuisance as the power soaked into me. It filled my skin until it overflowed, sliding in and through and over me, and I expanded with it.

Shaking off Tanith's clasp seemed almost like an afterthought.

Through the euphoria pouring out of me, a vibration thrummed into my underbelly, pounding across the ground, accompanied by a high-pitched howl.

Somehow, I knew it was Kade in his animal form, returning for me.

TWENTY-THREE

Wʜen the golden mongoose burst into the clearing, he skidded to a halt, taking in the scene in a quick glance. Scott lay crumpled against the cliff wall, either dead or unconscious. Tanith, on the other hand, was still very much alive, rearing back and hissing, watching every move I made, circling around the clearing.

I moved closer to Kade, and he stepped up to stand beside me, growling low in his throat.

Only then did I realize that Tanith had maneuvered herself close enough to Scott to wrap her lower body around his.

Using her shifter strength, she pulled him away from the cliff, hissing the whole time.

The Earth magic thrummed through me, tying me to Kade as he snarled, and I knew the moment we should strike, together.

His leap placed him on the back of Tanith's neck, even as I used my constrictor coils to rip Scott away from her again, and my viper fangs to tear into her throat.

The skin tore away from the bloody gouges we left, showing white and fleshy on the underside as we ripped it away from her.

In the end, Scott lay sobbing on the ground as we ripped his mother to shreds in front of him.

If he'd been anyone else, I might have felt sorry for him.

As it was, I felt as cold-blooded about it as any snake could.

She was a predator, and she needed to die. And once she was dead, the evidence of her giant serpentine body needed to be hidden—some of it buried, the rest of it hidden in the caves above.

I would have happily turned my attention to Scott once Tanith had been dismembered and the pieces disposed of, but Kade stopped me, shifting back to his human form and urging me to do the same. "Do you hear that? Someone's coming up the riverbed."

Even once I had changed back, I couldn't hear what Kade heard.

Mammal hearing might be nice. But today, I would take lamia power over it.

"What should we do?" I asked. I pulled my borrowed clothes out of the crevasse where I'd left them and donned them again.

I was getting used to being naked in front of Kade. Seemed like it might end up being a regular part of shifter life.

"We drag Carson to the cavern. Then I'll distract the hikers," Kade said, the corner of his mouth crooking up in a smile of unholy glee that was utterly at odds with the seriousness of his tone. "You get the women out of here. Eduardo should be on his way. He'll help."

"What about the police?" I asked. "Should we alert them?"

"No." The gold flecks in Kade's eyes began to churn—not like they did for me, but with the beginning of his shift. "We'll take care of it."

"*We* being you and me and Eduardo?"

"If we need to bring the rest of the Council in, we will." His shoulders twitched, and he rolled his head around with a crackling noise. "But first, we take those women out of their cages." The last word came out on a hiss, but he still pulled me to him and kissed me, hard, his lips against mine a promise.

"I'll meet you at the CAP-C," I said, then turned without waiting for an answer.

Inside the cave, the women were silent, watching me with big eyes.

"She's dead," I said. When no one responded, I began searching for a key. I knew PTSD when I saw it. It would take more than one lamia's death for these women to be okay again.

"There's a key inside that box," one woman finally said, pointing to a container across the room from her.

Once I'd found the key, I began moving around the room, unlocking cages.

Still the women simply sat inside.

"Come on," I whispered, pulling open the first cage door and reaching in to help the woman inside move out and stand up straight. She placed one hand against her back and stretched, her pregnant belly sticking out in front of her. Then she shivered, wrapping her arms around herself and rubbing her hands up and down to her shoulders.

I glanced around, searching for something to drape over her, finally spying a stack of towels in a corner. "There," I said, pointing at them as I moved toward the next cage. "Grab those and start handing them out." They weren't much, but maybe they could help stave off hypothermia.

To be honest, I was a little afraid to check inside the rest of the crates—not because I didn't know what I might find, but because I was fairly certain I did know what I would find.

I was right. As I moved from cage to cage, popping open the locks and guiding women out to stand close to the fire in the center of the room, I encountered more blank stares and haunted gazes than I cared to consider.

I might be taking them out of this room, but I wasn't sure I could ever take them out of the hell they were in.

I wasn't sure any counselor could.

But I was going to do my best to help find one who was willing to try.

In the end, there were ten of them, six visibly pregnant.

And the thing none of us knew hung heavy in the air: pregnant with what?

TWENTY-FOUR

J anice stepped forward and placed her hand lightly on my shoulder. "You don't have to stay, you know." The Council leader's dark brown eyes were kind, but her smile didn't quite meet them.

I licked my lips, tasting the air to see if she meant the words, but all I could capture were the various scents of anger, from disgust to rage, emanating from the small crowd around me. Shaking my head, I shrugged. "I need to see this through. I found him. I should be here…" My voice trailed off.

"When justice is done?" Eduardo's deep voice echoed from beside me. The Shield had indeed shown up at the cavern, just as I was leading the women up to the road at the top of the cliff. He, along with several other Council members, had been invaluable in the days since as we worked to help reintroduce the women into their world—and began introducing them into ours.

The children—the ones we had been able to save at the hotel, and Kirstie Bryant, as well—had all survived.

Janice dropped her hand. "Well, be warned. Shifter law

is not for the faint-hearted." She nodded at each of us in turn, then headed toward the knot of people surrounding Scott.

"I'm not even sure shifter law and justice are the same thing." Kade's warm hand settled into the small of my back, and I leaned into it, drawing comfort from the heat that poured from his body into mine. He swung a leather back-pack off his shoulder and dropped it at his feet.

"Maybe not," Eduardo said, "But it's the closest thing we have."

Kade tilted his other hand, palm open, toward the other man in a gesture that resembled acknowledgement, but also managed to convey doubt.

As the Shield slid into the group, slipping past people with barely a ripple, I turned into Kade's embrace. "I'm glad you're here," I said, keeping my voice low despite knowing that most of the shifters here could hear me perfectly well.

"I haven't decided whether I'm glad you're here," he replied, but his crooked smile took away any sting the words might have had otherwise. "But since you are, I'm glad I'm here with you." The gold flecks in his eyes churned slowly, and more of his body heat washed over me like a tide.

Some secret message seemed to move through the crowd at that moment, silencing everyone almost simultaneously. Like everyone around me, I turned my eyes toward the center of the clearing, where Janice had stepped up onto the makeshift stage of several large boulders moved into place by some of the stronger shifters.

"Welcome," she said, her middle-aged, motherly appearance at odds with the hardness of her tone. "We come together tonight to pass judgment upon Scott Carson. He is one of our own, accepted for his shifter blood, though not himself a shifter. The prisoner may rise."

Though his clothes were dirty and his broken bones, set and bandaged by Kade, meant that he sat in a straight-back chair rather than standing, Scott looked otherwise healthy —three days in one of his own cages had done him less harm than it had the women he had kept prisoner there.

The lack of regular, consistent beatings and rape had probably helped with that.

Rage welled up in my throat, and glittering Earth magic swirled around me. I pushed the incipient change back down.

Not yet.

Janice continued. "The Council has examined all the evidence gathered by our own Shields, by Dr. Kade Nevala, and by the lamia, Lindi Parker." A murmur swept through the crowd, and several heads swiveled toward me. I kept my eyes trained on Janice and the tableau in the clearing. Scott stared stoically ahead, not meeting anyone's gaze.

I wondered if he knew what was going to happen here tonight.

For just a moment, part of me mourned for the man I thought I had known. That man had believed in truth and in kindness. His easy laugh had charmed me, and his ready smile lifted my heart.

The man in this open-air court was not the one I had cared for.

This man was cruel, caring only for himself, for his grasp at power.

He wanted authority and control, but not the accompanying accountability.

And I was beginning to truly understand that the strength flowing through me with each shift came with a responsibility to those around me.

As Janice recited the long list of charges against Scott— kidnapping, rape, murder—an electric charge sparked through the air, jumping from shifter to shifter as the full extent of the prisoner's crimes became clear to everyone.

Diamante sparkles of magic began to swirl through the entire clearing, twirling around individual shifters in eddies of power that intensified with each word that Janice spoke. "In all of these charges, the Council finds Scott Carson guilty." Silver glints coalesced into steady streams of power coming together just above us. Janice ignored the light-show. "The sentence for these crimes is death, to be carried out immediately." As she pronounced the sentence, a bright light flashed above us, and power poured down onto us like a shower of glitter—but this glitter landed with a white-hot sizzle and sank down into my skin, leaving faint, luminous pinpricks behind.

I could feel it sinking down into my very core, infusing every part of me with power.

I knew I should probably be worried, but I couldn't help breathing in even more of the magic, drawing it into my lungs, letting it pulse through my veins and into my heart, feeling it burn into my bones.

The bright sheen across my eyesight came from inside.

This was what Scott had wanted—I could see the envy, the anger in his eyes as he watched the magic pass him by.

Too human.

I wondered how often his mother had told him he was too human to ever be enough for her.

For an instant, I felt sorry for him.

Then I remembered all the things he had done in his attempt to create the new lamia race his mother had so wanted, all the children he had murdered and women he had hurt, and the instant passed.

This was justice, no matter how ambivalent Kade felt about it.

From the center of the clearing, Janice turned to the

men guarding Scott and spoke again, her voice reverberating with new energy. "Let us begin." A circular wave of her hand over her head indicated all sides of the clearing, and a shimmering dome slipped into being around us.

That's when Scott began to struggle in earnest, screaming and struggling as the guards fought to hold him still.

Without thinking about it, I moved toward them. Kade's hand caught my upper arm, and I turned to stare into his eyes. "I can be the shift we need," I said, a small, sad smile tugging at one corner of my lips. After a searching gaze, he nodded and released me.

I touched one of the dome walls as I passed it. It was hard and cold, like glass, but a jolt of electricity shocked my fingers as I pulled them away.

Janice stood utterly still as I made my way to her. She didn't speak, but she met my eyes and gave one decisive nod. She stepped off the rock dais and two of the men Kade had pointed out as bear shifters at the Council meeting pulled the top boulder away, setting it off to the side. Then they joined the guards holding Scott, pulling him up from the chair and taking him to the now-flat rock pile, where they hoisted him atop the altar-shaped rock.

The only sounds inside the dome were Scott's renewed screams, bouncing off the glittering walls. Drawing on the new power inside me, I sank into the shift. The world turned gray and I felt my jaw unhinge as my tongue split. The ache in my teeth let me know when my fangs were ready.

I didn't finish the transformation. I didn't need to.

Circling behind Scott, I gestured to the men holding him to pull his arm straight and tilt his head to one side. One of the shifters ripped the prisoner's collar away from his shoulder. He resisted, but his human strength was no match for the shifters holding him.

Bending at the waist, I sought out the wild pulse at his neck, then moved away from it.

I didn't want him to die.

Not yet.

Finding the perfect spot, I reared back, then struck, my fangs springing down into my mouth as I moved, piercing Scott's flesh and pumping their venom out in waves.

After only a few seconds, I pulled myself back, some internal sensor warning me that any more might kill him.

Pushing down the euphoria that came with the strike, I forced myself to transform again. By the time I could speak again, Scott had stopped struggling, though his eyes rolled wildly from side to side.

"There," I said, panting with the exertion of two shifts so close together. "He'll be paralyzed for several hours, at least."

"We shouldn't need that long," Janice said.

I didn't look back as I made my way to Kade, grasping his hand tightly in my own and leaning my forehead against his.

"This is justice," I whispered. But I didn't know who I was trying to convince, Kade or myself. The were-mongoose simply squeezed my hands, then released them to pull me in close to him. I let him hug me for a moment before I turned around to face my actions.

The dome held us all there until it was done, and I forced myself to watch all of it.

The families of the murdered shifter children went first.

They started with his thumbs.

Because of my paralyzing venom, he couldn't even scream. By the time almost every member of the shifter community present had moved past the prisoner, there was barely an inch of Scott's body that had not been sliced, removed, or mutilated.

The shifters were remarkably organized, moving in an orderly line, each person partially shifting and inflicting one injury, none quite lethal. Claws and teeth were their only weapons.

To their credit, none of them appeared to relish the task.

I might have vomited, otherwise—or fainted.

Scott had passed out repeatedly, but each time, Janice had drawn on the shimmering magic surrounding us, and he had regained consciousness. His blood poured down the sides of the rock, and yet, because of my venomous bite, he could do no more than twitch in agony.

No one spoke.

Kade didn't take his gaze off the human being tortured to death, but he didn't participate in it, either.

When the last member of the winding line had solemnly inflicted a final horrific injury by using a single claw to slice a circle around Scott's left eyebrow and peel it from his face, Kade stepped forward. "Enough," he said. "Let it be done."

Janice gazed around the clearing, as if waiting for dissent. Finding none, she nodded. "It is done," she said.

At that, Kade sprang into action, grabbing the backpack he had dropped earlier and pushing through the other shifters until he reached the human at the altar. "Untie him," he said to the guards, who had remained motionless during the whole ceremony. The biggest of them, one of the bear shifters, moved first, his enormous fingers surprisingly nimble as they plucked at the knot in the rope.

"You'll have to hold him," Kade said, unzipping the backpack. "He can't balance himself." Pulling out a pre-filled syringe, he leaned over so Scott could see his face. "Scott? Can you hear me? Do you understand what I'm saying? Just blink if you understand." Then he blanched as he realized that at some point Scott's eyelids had been carefully removed. But Scott's eyes were tracking Kade, and their twitching seemed to indicate understanding.

"I'm going to give you something to make the pain go away," Kade said, tapping the syringe to check the contents, then sliding the needle carefully into the bloody remains of Scott's arm.

The maimed human's eyes rolled up into his head and the quivering attempts at movement finally stopped as he once again lost consciousness. This time, Janice allowed him to remain so.

Kade stared down at the man, his jaw tightening as he squared his shoulders.

"What now?" I asked.

"Now I kill him," the doctor said, bending down to pull a second syringe from his bag, then stopping again.

I didn't think anyone else could see the slight tremor in Kade's hand.

I stared down at the motionless form on the altar-rock, little more than a limp, bloody rag at this point. I didn't feel any more anger. I knew that I should have felt pity, but I didn't even have that left.

"Do it," I said.

Kade didn't wait for Janice's okay. He simply slid another needle into Scott, and with a final sigh, the criminal who had terrorized the shifter community blew out his last breath.

CHAPTER

TWENTY-FIVE

"Do we have any evidence at all that Scott was the killer?" I asked Kade. "Or will this just end up as another cold case?"

He shrugged. "If nothing else, the families of the children know they got justice."

I considered the statement. Before the last few days, I would have said that I didn't believe in the death penalty, that it was too harsh, too cruel, too inhumane. Too close to the things my snake-self wanted to see done.

Now?

Now I wasn't sure what counted as *inhumane*.

Or maybe even *inhuman*.

After all, Scott had been the only human involved, and of everyone I'd ever met, he had been the least humane. The least kind, the least forgiving. The least human.

I knew that some of the Council members might have argued that Scott's lamia blood was to blame for his cruelty.

My counselor training told me it was nurture, not

nature—that his mother had trained him into a ruthless killer.

Neither answer seemed entirely satisfactory. And my training and experience told me that they never would be. There is no good excuse for people who can hurt children. Scott's parentage complicated the question, but didn't offer any answers, only more questions.

A WEEK LATER, Kade picked me up after work to take me to another Council meeting. It was the third time he had come to work to get me. Everyone at the CAP-C assumed we were dating. But whatever was going on with us was far from anything so simple or straightforward. The attraction between us still simmered under the surface, occasionally flaring up into something more tangible.

Whenever he looked at me with those swirling golden eyes, it sent a bolt of heat straight through me—and as often as not, my own vision grayed out and I had to fight to maintain control over my human form.

I saw him struggling, too.

But we hadn't done anything about it recently.

I expected Kade was still angry about the disagreement we'd had, perhaps even more about my decision to go home with Scott that night, but he didn't come out and say so.

I didn't ask, either.

So whatever was between us just bubbled along underneath our interactions, inflecting every look, every word, every accidental brushing of our fingertips against one another. Eventually, we would have to deal with it—with *us*.

But not tonight.

This evening, we were meeting with the Council to

decide what to do about me.

I didn't belong. Not really.

The shapeshifters lived in groups, in tiny enclaves like the bobcats' clowder, all their homes grouped together. The various clans had territory, and rules, and a definite pecking order.

I was a clan of one. Not a clan at all. Not right now, anyway. Some of the human women in Scott's breeding program had opted to continue their pregnancies, despite the horrific trauma, after Kade reassured them that any children would be taken in by the Council.

The birth of another lamia therefore remained a distinct possibility.

I wouldn't wish this life on anyone, but the thought of never being so alone again appealed to me, just as it had when Tanith had offered it to me. I might know why I felt that way—virtually every abandoned or orphaned child wished for family, and I had gone through plenty of counseling for it as I pursued my degree, but neither academic nor self-knowledge could completely eliminate that desire.

But this night's meeting was about my place in the larger group of the clans, not about any smaller clan I might want to create.

Once again, I stood in the center of a group of shapeshifters in Janice's living room.

"Okay, everyone," the Council leader said. "Let's get started." She waved for attention, then read from a sheet of typewritten paper in her hand.

"We are here to complete the record of Scott Carson, human, lamia-born, sentenced and executed for the crimes of kidnapping, rape, and murder, particularly killing shifters without Shield or Sanction of the Council."

Then she read the names of all the shifters Scott had killed.

At the end, she read the date of Scott's death aloud, then asked of the room at large, "Does anyone have anything to add?"

Here was the part Kade had warned me about—the part where they got to decide if I could join them. Or even be left alone to live my life.

"You're something new. It's totally unprecedented for a lamia to want to be part of the Council," Kade had said the night before. "There will be some shifters who want to block you from membership. We need to get you voted in while your role in taking Scott down is still fresh in everyone's mind. Before any of the old guard has a chance to gather support."

I wasn't even sure I wanted to be part of the Council, but apparently, refusal wasn't really an option, not if I wanted to continue to live my life unmolested by rabid lamia-haters.

Rabid in a metaphorical sense. Who knew if werewolves carried rabies for real?

My snarky inner voice insisted on offering commentary as I stood up with Kade and moved to stand with him, next to Janice.

"Tonight," the leader continued. "We also vote on whether to accept the lamia Lindi Parker into the Council as representative of Clan Lamia."

I knew there had been a lot of debate about this behind the scenes. Accepting me meant accepting the possibility of an eventual, actual Clan Lamia. Especially if any of Scott's forced offspring were viable snake shifters.

In fact, several of the Council members had argued to have any lamia babies peremptorily euthanized. I had argued against that vehemently. I wasn't certain how seriously they had taken me.

But any of those offspring would be babies—and not

just snake babies, but human ones. As trainable as I was.

I had to believe that they could be saved, could be part of this community of shifters.

Otherwise, we were nothing more than our animal selves, and every part of me—even the snake part—rebelled against the idea that I was no more than my inner reptile.

Janice had responded by asking if I was prepared to stand in as a parent to any lamia children—and I couldn't very well say no. No one was better trained for it, between my personal experience as a lamia and my professional training as a children's counselor.

Even now, I couldn't decide if I wanted to become an instant mother to a clutch of human-snake hybrid babies, or if I would rather go on being the only one—maybe the last one—of my kind.

In the end, almost half of the Council members had argued against my inclusion in their ranks, so strongly that the Council had finally decided to put it to an open vote.

As I stood there trying to prepare for the vote, the anxious scents in the living room intensified, now identifiable to me as shifter-scent from nervous human/hybrids. Primarily mammals.

For once, Kade's spicy scent read to me as comfort.

I steeled myself for a long, hard verbal battle when Hank, the heckler from my first Council visit, climbed to his feet and took a breath to speak.

But then Eduardo Valencia, the fighter Kade had pointed out as a Shield, the man who had later stepped in to help me fight Scott and Tanith, also stood.

"Madam Chairperson." Eduardo nodded at her, then at Kade and me. "I wish to speak."

From the looks on everyone's faces, this level of formality was unusual for the Shield. All around me, shifters held their breath, their eyes focused on Eduardo. I glanced curiously at Kade, who made the slightest motion with one finger, letting me know that he'd answer questions later without ever taking his intense stare off of the other man.

Eduardo continued in his slow, measured voice. "I speak now as First Shield."

A collective gasp went up from the room. I frowned, trying to read the flavor of the room. Anxious, definitely. Frightened, perhaps? Excited even?

Janice nodded. "Yes." Her voice took on an even more formal cadence. "Do the Shields wish to maintain their protection of this lamia?"

A sudden grin creased Eduardo's face, the lines around his eyes almost hiding their twinkle.

"No, ma'am," he drawled. "The Shields wish to recruit this lamia."

It took several seconds for Janice to regain control of the room. "You wish to train the lamia Lindi Parker as a Shield?"

If I hadn't been standing next to her, I might not have caught it as she glanced at me and her eyelid shivered downward just a little in the barest hint of a wink at me.

Holy crap. This was a set-up.

"We do. Lindi already works with the human police in matters of human crime, and with human children and their families in matters of pain. We believe she will be a valuable addition to the Shields." As he spoke, several other people throughout the room began to move, gathering around him until they formed a semi-circle facing me.

The other Shields, I presumed.

Janice watched the group converging to stand with the First Shield, and turned toward me. "Lindi, does this work for you?" When she asked, she dropped the formal tone.

Did it? They wanted me to—what? Be the counselor for the shapeshifter Council?

"I don't even know what a Shield does," I finally protested, albeit weakly.

"We'll teach you," Eduardo said, his chocolate-brown eyes oddly intense on mine. He wanted me to say yes, very badly.

Flicking my gaze to Kade, I waited for him to send me some signal to let me know that this was a bad idea.

Instead, when he looked from Eduardo's face to mine, he gave me a single, curt nod.

If anyone was likely to advise against it, it would be Kade.

I drew in a deep breath, squared my shoulders, stared Janice in the eyes, and said in as firm a voice as I could manage, "Yes. I will join the Shields."

About half the room seemed to exhale in relief. The rest of the inhabitants virtually exuded anger. A low growl undercut the smattering of applause.

Eduardo held up his hand in what was apparently some sort of oath. "Then as First Shield, I will hereby take your vow."

Nodding, I followed his example, and repeated the simple words after him. "I hereby swear to honor and protect the Council, its members, and all the shifter clans, to act as a Shield against any that would offer harm. This I will do in the name of all that is good and right."

As I finished the oath, Janice gently gestured me back into the group. "Excellent. Now that's settled, we can move on to other matters.

I let Kade lead me to a corner, where I discovered that my knees were shaking.

I hadn't realized exactly how much of the tension I had absorbed from the room.

"What was that?" I hissed, pulling Kade into the small vestibule leading to the front door.

"The Shields police their own," the mongoose shifter whispered. "If you're one of them, the rest of the Council can't touch you."

"Did you know that was going to happen?"

"Not a clue."

"Any downsides?" Our hastily whispered conversation was starting to get some glares from the nearest shifters, but I needed information now.

Kade chewed on his lip. "They're absolutely scrupulous about their own behavior. They have to be. The Shields will turn one of their own over in a heartbeat. Other than that? Nothing."

"So they follow a code?"

"A strict one."

I could do that. It didn't sound too far from my ethical responsibilities as a counselor.

But my job...

"Can I stay at the CAP-C?" I asked.

Kade shrugged. "Talk to Eduardo. But most of us have mundane jobs, no matter what we do for the Council."

Okay. I could do this.

I could really be a member of the Council.

I turned my attention back to the meeting in progress. I had half-expected the Council to take up the issue of the potential lamia babies, but instead, Janice closed out the meeting without ever bringing them up.

Apparently, they really were going to be left to me.

As the crowd began to break up, more than one shifter snarled at me on the way out.

None of them dared cross the Shields by doing more, though.

I hung back, waiting for a chance to speak to Janice.

Instead, Eduardo approached me and drew me away from Kade to hand me a business card that had only his name, phone number, and email address.

"Tomorrow," he said, "we begin your training."

"I work until almost six o'clock," I said.

The older man's nod suggested he already knew this. "At eight o'clock," he said. "In the Holy Circle, where the doctor took you to train." Without another word, he strolled away.

I watched the First Shield melt into the small crowd of people who remained, chatting in Janice's front yard.

Some of them were still scowling at me, angry at the Shield's move to protect me, but more—many more—were stopping to say hello, to greet me. To welcome me into their world.

For the first time ever, I realized, I felt like those greetings were possibly true.

Real.

Accepting.

Like I might actually learn to belong here, with these people.

Kade stepped up beside me and took my hand in his. "You okay?" he asked.

His spicy scent, warm and safe and exciting, all at once, enveloped me, and I leaned into him, not caring who saw us kiss.

"Yes," I said, a long time later as I finally pulled my mouth from his. "I think I'm going to be just fine."

Love Lindi and Kade? Want to see what happens next? Be sure to read Book 2 of the series, The Skin She's In!

AUTHOR'S NOTE

Readers familiar with North Central Texas will notice that I've taken some liberties with the geography of the area, setting part of the story in caverns not far from Dinosaur Valley in Glen Rose, Texas. No such deep caves exist, though there are shallow caves that show evidence of Native American habitation overlooking the Brazos and Paluxy Rivers. Similarly, descriptions of the Paluxy River vary in some detail from the actual river's course.

ACKNOWLEDGMENTS

There are always people to thank for helping with the technical aspects of a book—and I am certainly thankful to all of them (I hope I remembered everyone in the list below!)—but for this book, in particular, it has been the love and kindness and generosity of the people in my world who have made it possible. Perhaps more than any other I've written, this book is a work of my heart. I wrote it at a time when my world was changing faster than I could keep up, and often in unpredictable and frightening ways. My family, my friends, and writing were often all that kept me steady. In no particular order, I would like to thank my parents, Isabel, Don and Debbie, Daniel and Allison, Lateia, Erin, Eli, Amber, Bokerah, Melanie, Emily, Kimberly, Clint, Jim, Pamela and Michael, Deborah, Gary and Lisa, Allessandria, Shelley, Robin, and Jennifer. You all make my life a better place to be. I love you all.

ABOUT THE AUTHOR

USA Today, *Wall Street Journal*, and *New York Times* bestselling author **Margo Bond Collins** is a former college English professor who, tired of explaining the difference between "hanged" and "hung," turned to writing romance novels instead. Sometimes her heroines kill monsters, sometimes they kiss aliens. But they always aim for the heart!

Want to hang out with the author, win book prizes, see the cool covers first, and support Margo's books on social media? Join The Vampirarchy, Margo's street team on Facebook!

MORE BOOKS BY MARGO

Urban Fantasy and Paranormal Romance

Tessa Fury, Accidental Bounty Hunter

Midlife Monsters

Midnight's Assassins

Lindi Parker, Shifter Shield Series

Science-Fiction Romance

Interstellar Shifters

Khanavai Warriors Alien Bride Games Series

Her Alien Crew

Galactic Gladiator Games

Contemporary Romance

Depraved

Kings of Clubs

JOIN MARGO ONLINE

www.MargoBondCollins.net
Bookbub
Facebook
Twitter
Instagram
Amazon